Stage Fright

STAGE FRIGHT

A Sebastian Barth Mystery by

JAMES HOWE

Atheneum 1986 *New York*

Library of Congress Cataloging-in-Publication Data

Howe, James.   Stage fright.

(Sebastian Barth mysteries)
SUMMARY: Young Sebastian Barth investigates the
tangle of warnings and ominous accidents surrounding
a famous actress visiting his home town.
[1. Actors and actresses—Fiction.   2. Mystery
and detective stories]   I. Title.   II. Series.
PZ7.H83727St   1986   [Fic]   85-20025
ISBN 0-689-31160-5

Stage Fright

1 "YOU MUST BE SEBASTIAN," said the actress in a voice the boy recognized from about a million movies. Her eyes, which seemed to know him though they'd just met, were pools of melted blue ice.

I must be dreaming, he thought.

But he wasn't. Michaele Caraway, *the* Michaele Caraway, was standing on the sidewalk in front of his house, *his* house in Pembroke, Connecticut, holding his hand in hers. He felt his palms begin to sweat.

"Is your mother home? She is expecting me, isn't she?"

Sebastian nodded. "She's out back. We thought you were coming this afternoon."

"I was eager to get here," Michaele said, releasing Sebastian's hand. "It's been ages since Katie and I have seen each other. How old are you, Sebastian?"

"Thirteen."

"There, you see," said Michaele. "It's been at least thirteen years. I've never even met you. And Katie's never met . . ." The actress looked around her as if she'd dropped a glove. "Where— Donovan. Donovan!"

[3]

Expecting a tiny French poodle to pop out of the car parked at the curb, Sebastian was surprised to see instead the face of a boy of nine or ten loom into view in the frame of the front, right window.

Michaele laughed and shook her head. "Were you hiding, love?" she asked. "Don't be shy. This is Sebastian. I'm sure you and he will be great friends."

"Hi," Sebastian said.

The boy pushed open the car door and emerged slowly. "Hi," he said, looking down at the grass.

Just then, another door opened and through it came Sebastian's mother. She ran down the front steps of the house. "Michaele!" she cried. "You look wonderful. I wasn't expecting you so soon. Look at me, I'm a mess. You're so . . . so radiant. You *look* like a movie star, I swear. To think we were once roommates. Sebastian, did I tell you that Michaele and I were roommates in college?"

"Only about a hundred times," Sebastian said, throwing a smile Donovan's way. It missed the boy, who was still staring at the ground.

"Katie, stop rambling," said Michaele. "God, I wish I didn't make people so nervous."

"And this is your son," Katie said.

"This is Donovan."

"Well, I'm pleased to meet you, Donovan," said Katie. "I'm so happy that you and your mom have come to stay with us." When Donovan didn't reply, Katie turned to her son and said, "Sebastian, why

[4]

don't you help Donovan feel at home while I catch up on old times with Michaele?"

Sebastian watched his mother put her arm through Michaele's and walk up the stairs to the house. Suddenly Michaele tossed her head and laughed just the way she had in *The Best of Enemies* when Robert Redford had asked her, "How are you, anyway?" "Anyway, I'm fine," she'd said. "But *this* way, I'm best of all." And then she'd kissed him. On the lips.

To Sebastian's surprise, his mother asked Michaele the same question now.

"How are you, anyway?" she said, holding the front door open.

Was it because they'd walked into the shade, or did Michaele's face really lose its color at that moment? Sebastian listened carefully to her answer, which was little more than a whisper.

"Terrified," she said.

2 "I'M TERRIFIED, truly," Michaele said that night at dinner. "I haven't been on the stage in years. I don't know how I let Cliff convince me to come up here and do this little play of his."

Will Barth, Sebastian's father, passed Michaele the vegetables, which she accepted so graciously the bowl might have been filled with rosebuds rather than broccoli. Will's face colored slightly; Katie smiled.

"Perhaps this 'little play' of Cliff's will be a hit," Katie said. "It could end up on Broadway—and you with it."

"That's possible," said Michaele, "though I'm not sure that's what I want. What I need is a chance to test myself. I've been making movies for such a long time now that people have forgotten I can *act*. *I've* forgotten I can act. I mean, the Spider Lady in *Insectivore* isn't exactly what one would call acting."

"I saw that movie," said Sebastian. "I thought it was neat. Especially the part where the giant mole—"

"I'm glad you liked it," Michaele said. "It was very popular. Alas. But, the point is—"

"The point is you want to do some *real* acting," said Katie. "And that's what you've come to our little summer stock theater to do."

"Exactly." Turning to Sebastian, Michaele said, "Your mother tells me you have a part in the play."

Sebastian shrugged. "They're using local kids for the children's parts. I was lucky to be chosen."

"No false modesty," Michaele said. "Dougie Scott wouldn't cast someone without talent. You're playing my son, yes?"

He nodded.

"Sebastian does have talent," said his grandmother. "He's a very bright young man."

"I'm sure he is," Michaele said.

"He has his own radio program, did you know that?"

"Gram . . ."

"No, I didn't."

"Oh, yes," Jessica Hallem went on, despite Sebastian's protests. "It's a talk show for young listeners. And it's on every week. I never miss it."

"That's because you're a young listener, Gram," said Sebastian.

"Thank you, dear." Turning back to Michaele, Jessica said, "He's a detective, too, you know."

"Is he?" Michaele said.

Donovan, who had been silent during most of the meal, looked at Sebastian with interest.

"Oh, yes," said Jessica. "He has solved quite a

[7]

number of puzzling mysteries about town."

"A young Sherlock Holmes, eh?" Michaele said.

"You may laugh," Sebastian's grandmother went on, "but I'm quite serious. He's an astute observer of human nature. Surprisingly so, for a person his age."

"That quality will serve him as an actor, too," Michaele said. "I can only hope he won't need it as a detective. I'm nervous enough about this production without having a mystery thrown in."

"I like mysteries," Donovan said softly.

"Solving them?" Will asked. "Or creating them?"

Everyone laughed. Everyone, that is, but Donovan.

"Tell me, Michaele," said Jessica. "Whatever happened to Douglas Scott? You said that he's directing the play, didn't you?"

Michaele nodded.

"He was an awfully successful director at one time," Jessica said. "Then, poof! One heard nothing of him."

"He had a string of bad luck," Michaele said slowly. "One rotten play after another. Soon no one would touch him. It's a shame, really. He's such a talented man. And so dear. He was like a second father to me when I was starting out. He directed my first play on Broadway, you see. But it's a fickle busi-

[8]

ness. And luck has so much to do with success."

"More than talent?" Will asked.

"It takes both," said Michaele. "And some magic ingredient that's added when the two coincide."

"Sounds mystical," Jessica said, helping herself to some boiled potatoes.

"In a way, it is." Michaele fell silent for a moment. Then, turning to Sebastian, she asked, "Are you looking forward to rehearsals starting tomorrow?"

"A lot," Sebastian said. "I can't believe we only have a week though."

"That's summer stock," said Michaele. "Will you ride out to the theater with Donovan and me in the morning?"

"Sure."

The telephone rang.

"It may be for me," Michaele said, as Sebastian jumped up to get it. "I'm expecting Dougie to call."

"That's who it is," Sebastian said, handing the phone to Michaele. He was blushing.

"Hello, love," Michaele said into the phone. "How's my favorite director?"

"What's the matter?" Katie asked her son.

"Nothing," he said.

"Oh, come on."

Sebastian looked to be sure Michaele wasn't listening. "He called me 'darling,'" he said.

Katie smiled. "That's summer stock," she said.

[9]

3 THAT NIGHT, Sebastian had trouble falling asleep. All he could think about was the fact that he was going to be in a real play with a real actress, a movie star. Summer was coming to an end, school would be starting soon, but none of that mattered right now. For the next two weeks, he was going to be Michaele Caraway's son.

Every few minutes, he turned on the lamp by his bed and picked up the script lying next to it. He opened it but didn't read. He simply wanted to remind himself that it was real, all of it real.

At quarter past twelve, he put down the script for the last time and turned out the light. Yawning, he tried to imagine what the next day would bring. One thing he knew for certain: he had to be up at six o'clock to deliver newspapers, rehearsal or no rehearsal. He wondered how many famous actors had had newspaper routes when they were young. He imagined himself laughing about it years later, telling an interviewer in an offhand way, "Sure, I had a paper route once."

"Really?" he heard the interested interviewer ask. "Tell us about it, Sebastian."

He was getting drowsy and couldn't hear his reply. But he knew that he was being witty and charming. He knew because he heard the sound of laughter and applause. And it was that sound that lulled him to sleep at last.

4 AFTER FINISHING his paper route the next morning, Sebastian pedaled his bike as fast as he could to David Lepinsky's house. He often joined his best friend's family for breakfast.

"So," said David's father, as Sebastian came up the back porch stairs, "a star is born."

Pushing the screen door open, Sebastian entered the kitchen. He smiled at Josh Lepinsky and the smell of bacon. "I don't know about that," he said. "It isn't such a big part. At least, I don't think it is."

Josh broke several eggs into a frying pan. "You mean you haven't counted your lines?" he asked. "Rachel has not only counted her lines, she's counted her words. If I hadn't stopped her, she would have tabulated her letters and punctuation marks." Rachel, who was David's younger sister, had been cast in the play as well.

"I'm not quite that obsessive," said Sebastian.

Josh tossed the eggshells into the sink and wiped his hands on his apron, the one that read "This Chef Accepts Compliments."

"Are you excited?" he asked Sebastian.

Sebastian nodded. "Nervous too," he said. "I've never been in a play before. Except when I was a monkey in fourth grade. But I didn't have to say anything."

"True, but your scratching was very convincing."

"Thank you."

"You're welcome." The contents of the frying pan sizzled and popped. "Where are those children of mine? I will serve no egg after its time."

Josh went to the bottom of the hall stairs and hollered up, "Hey, you two. Get a move on."

Returning to the kitchen, he said, "So you've gone from playing a monkey to playing Michaele Caraway's son. Not to mention Rachel Lepinsky's brother. That's some career move, my boy."

Sebastian laughed. "I know."

"What's this big movie star like, anyway? I've only seen her from afar. Despite the fact that we live across the street from each other, Sebastian, no one in your house has seen fit to introduce her to the dashingly handsome—and available, I might add—bachelor father in this house. And she's been in town for twenty-four hours already, for cripes' sake." Josh glanced at the clock. "I lied. Twenty-one hours and seventeen minutes."

Sebastian started to answer Josh when David and Rachel appeared. "It's about time," said Josh, lifting the frying pan from the stove.

"No eggs for me," Rachel said. Her face was covered with something thick and wet and green. "I'll have half a grapefruit. I'm watching my calories. In my business, you have to, you know."

"What's your business?" David asked. "Scaring babies?"

"What *is* that on your face?" said Josh. "You look like a chemistry experiment gone haywire."

"It's smushed avocado," Rachel said with disdain, as if the answer were obvious. "It helps keep wrinkles away."

"Rachel," Josh said, "you're nine years old. Wrinkles are much too busy sneaking up on old people like me to be bothered with anyone your age. Now, go upstairs and remove the avocado. Never mind that I was planning to use it in a salad tonight. And hurry up, because your eggs are getting cold and mean."

Rachel began to pout. "Oh, Dad," she said. "You just don't understand actors."

"Of course I don't understand actors," said Josh. "I'm still trying to understand children."

"Oh, Dad."

"Go."

After breakfast, Rachel excused herself to do what she called vocal warm-ups, leaving her brother and Sebastian to do the dishes.

"Just think," David said, as the sink filled with

sudsy water. "For the next two weeks, she'll be *your* bratty kid sister instead of mine."

"Yeah, but you get Donovan."

"Who's Donovan?"

"Michaele Caraway's son. He's going to be hanging out with you guys."

"You mean, the apprentices?"

"Yeah. His mom thought it would keep him happy. I think it's just going to make everybody else miserable."

"Why? What's wrong with him?"

"Nothing serious. He's nine."

"Rachel's age. Funny, I don't remember it being so bad when we were nine."

"All I can tell you is that I spent most of yesterday afternoon trying to entertain him. This kid's idea of fun is squashing bugs."

"Oh," said David. "At least Rachel's nonviolent."

There was a knock on the back door. David and Sebastian turned to see their friend, Corrie Wingate, standing on the porch. Sebastian waved her in. "Hi," he said. "Are you all set to start apprenticing?"

Corrie nodded. "I'm really excited about it," she said. "Listen, do you want a ride to the theater? My mom's driving Buster and me out in about an hour."

"Sebastian and I are riding our bikes," said David.

"Actually," Sebastian said, not looking directly at his friends, "I'm going with Michaele."

"Michaele Caraway?" Corrie asked. David said nothing.

Sebastian wasn't sure why he felt a little sheepish, but he did. "She asked me to go with her last night, and I said yes. Besides, she doesn't know how to get to Siddons," he said, referring to Siddons College, where the theater was located.

"Gee," Corrie said, "you're going to be riding with a movie star."

"Sebastian says she's not like a movie star," said David. "He says she's like a real person."

"I can't wait to meet her," Corrie said. "I almost wish I were in the play. Except that it would make me a nervous wreck. This way I get to help out and be around, but I don't have to go out there onstage and make a fool of myself. Doesn't that make you nervous, Sebastian?"

"Making a fool of myself?"

Corrie laughed. "That didn't come out the way I meant it," she said. "Listen, I've got to go. I'll see you guys later." She hurried out the door, then poked her head back in. "Oh, Sebastian," she said.

"Yeah?"

"Good luck."

"Thanks," said Sebastian, smiling. "I'll try not to make a fool of myself."

5 MICHAELE'S EYES were closed. Her right hand fidgeted with a bent nail. At length, her hand grew still and her eyes slowly opened. She turned to Sebastian, seated next to her, and smiled.

"I was praying to Saint Genesius," she whispered, "the patron saint of actors. It's something I do whenever I start a new project."

Sebastian looked around the long, rectangular table at the faces of the others gathered this day on the stage of the Siddons College Auditorium to begin rehearsals for the world premiere of *The House of Cards*, A Serious Comedy by Cliff Davies.

His gaze came to rest on the playwright, scrunched so tightly in his chair at the far end of the table that he looked as though he'd been screwed into place. His eyes peered out from between a feathery spray of fallen hair and a pair of owlish tortoise-shell glasses resting halfway down his nose. He seemed to be spying on the world. Sebastian thought that that was perhaps what a writer was: a spy, but one who revealed the secrets he'd observed. Davies' hands, resting on the table, seemed more the hands of a laborer—large and worn and rough. The only thing that gave them away as being a writer's were the nails, which were bitten to the quick.

The director came into view then, stopping at the playwright's chair to speak with him. Sebastian had grown fond of the odd-looking, little man already. He liked the way he had asked everyone to call him Dougie and had made each member of the cast, young and old, feel as if he belonged. "The theater is a family," Dougie Scott had said earlier that morning. "We are all in this together."

Sebastian looked around him now at the other actors in the play. Next to him was Michaele, whose hands had gone back to toying with the bent nail. He wondered at its significance. On the other side of her was Rachel Lepinsky, his stage sister. Sebastian had to smile remembering all the times he'd left David's house glad that he was an only child.

Across the table sat Mark Lawson, the handsome star of a daytime soap opera called "Love on the Fast Track." His habit of breaking into a toothy smile and running his fingers through his curly black hair made it appear that he was perpetually waiting for a photographer from *People* magazine to show up. In an attempt to befriend Sebastian, the actor had spent a good part of the morning slapping him playfully on the back and saying things like, "Hey, big guy, what do you think of those Red Sox?" Sebastian, who thought very little about those Red

Sox, had known Mark for less than an hour, but he thought if he was called "big guy" one more time, he'd get sick all over Mark's snakeskin boots.

Mark had the role of Jason Card, Michaele's upstairs neighbor and, as it turns out, a former husband. In the play, Jason has three children from a second marriage. Sebastian was looking at two of them now. Liz and Sarah Burke were sisters in real life. Sebastian guessed Liz's age to be fifteen. He knew that Sarah was thirteen because she was in his class at school. Sarah, chewing gum (an entire pack, from the look of it), appeared to be bored. Sebastian knew her well enough to recognize the look as a cover for something else—nervousness, perhaps, or the fear of not being seen as cool. Liz, on the other hand, was harder to read. She was staring at Michaele Caraway in a vague sort of way that could have suggested anything from awe to contempt.

Next to Liz was an empty chair, belonging to the third stage child of Mark Lawson. Sebastian observed its intended occupant playing near the edge of the stage. Buster Wingate, Corrie's five-year-old brother, appeared far more interested at the moment in how close he could get his racing car to *vroom* to the stage's edge without falling off than in rehearsing a play.

Also in the cast were two stage actors from New York City: Doris Carpenter, playing Michaele's sister, and Rob McGrath, playing Mark Lawson's best friend. They were huddled together, whispering and laughing like old chums, which they might well have been. Sebastian didn't have time to observe them longer, as the voice of the stage manager brought the actors' break to an end.

"All right, everybody," called Mintsy Jones, so-called because of her love of chocolate-covered mints, "your five minutes are up."

Everyone laughed, since the five-minute break they had been given was in fact closer to twenty. The director took his place at the table, picking up his script of *The House of Cards* and clearing his throat.

"Thank you, Mintsy," he said. "Now, everyone, you listen to the stage manager when she talks." He looked into the eyes of the younger members of the cast. "She's the boss around here. Think of her as your mother."

Mintsy let out a whoop. "I'm only twenty-three!" she cried.

"Think of her as an older sister," said a new voice, with an English accent. "You can think of me as your mum."

Everyone turned to see a pleasant-looking woman with sandy hair, standing in an aisle of the auditorium.

"Ah, Sally," Dougie Scott said. "What a pleasure. Come on up. Let me introduce you to the cast."

"I can't stay a minute," said the woman named

Sally. "I've just come round to let everyone know they should pop over to the costume shop after rehearsal today so I can fit them up for the play. You'll let everyone know where to find me, Mintsy, will you?"

"Of course," Mintsy said. "Just follow the smell of tea. Sally always has the kettle on."

Again, the company laughed, Sally with them. "I'll see you all later," she said, waving her hand and disappearing up the aisle into the darkened theater. The director turned back to his actors.

"Now," he said. "Shall we begin? Sebastian, you have the first line. Remember, everyone, that today we are simply reading the play. No one is to *act*, do you understand? Just say the words. There will be time for acting soon enough. Mintsy, the stage directions, please."

Mintsy picked up her script and read in a loud voice. " 'A two-story house. On the upper level, Jason Card is seen watching television with his five-year-old son, Alexander. On the lower level, the front door to the house opens. A teenage boy, Jonathan Dexter, enters. His mother, Heather, and younger sister, Jenny, follow. Putting down the boxes they're carrying, they look around at their new home. They don't look pleased.' "

" 'Boy, Mom,' " said Sebastian, reading from the script, " 'what a dump!' "

6 "HOW DID IT GO?" David asked when he saw his friend enter the scenery shop late that afternoon. He had to speak loudly to be heard over the din made by the dozen or so apprentices engaged in their labors.

"I'm pooped," Sebastian said, glancing around the large, barnlike room. He saw some familiar faces among the apprentices; others he did not recognize. Spotting Corrie, he waved. "We did a lot in one day. But I guess we had to. We only have six rehearsals left. I looked for you guys at lunchtime. Where were you?"

"We went with Richard to the lumberyard."

"Who's Richard?"

David pointed to a tall, bearded man sawing wood. "He's the TD," he said.

"TD?"

"Technical Director. He tells us slaves what to do."

"You don't seem to be working that hard."

"Look at these hands," David cried, holding up his palms. "What do you see?"

"You'll have a long life and marry a lady with a moustache," said Sebastian.

"Very funny. Blisters. Look, I have blisters. You want to see what we did today?"

Just then, Corrie came over. "Hi," she said. "Did you have a good rehearsal?"

Sebastian nodded. "In the morning, we had a read-through. Then we talked about what we'd read, discussed our characters and stuff like that. After lunch, we blocked the play."

"What's that mean?" asked Corrie.

"The director tells you where to move when you say your lines, and you write it down in your script. In shorthand, sort of. And then we were measured for our costumes."

"Wow," Corrie said. "It all sounds so neat. We spent the day building flats."

"I was just going to show Sebastian," said David.

"What are flats?"

David pointed to a stack of tall wooden frames leaning against a wall. "They have to be covered with muslin yet," he said. "We just put together the frames."

"What do they do?"

"When they're all covered and painted, they'll be the walls of the house."

"Oh," Sebastian said, nodding. "That makes sense. Listen, do you guys want a ride home? Michaele's leaving in a few minutes. I told her I'd get Donovan. Where is he, anyway?"

"There," David said, pointing to a corner of the room where Donovan sat grappling with a hammer. "He was getting in everybody's way, so Richard told him to take the nails out of all those old pieces of wood."

"He's been at it for hours," Corrie said. Then, "Thanks for the offer, Sebastian, but my mom is picking me up. I'm supposed to go shopping with her. I wish I could meet Michaele Caraway, though."

"Come over to my house tonight, and you will."

"Really?"

"Sure."

"Oh, neat. Listen, I've got to go. I'll see you tonight."

After Corrie left, David said, "I have my bike, Sebastian, remember? Besides, I have to ride home with Rachel."

"Oh, yeah, I forgot. Well, I'd better get the kid and head for Michaele's dressing room. I'm meeting her there."

"Can I go with you? I have this package I'm supposed to deliver to her."

"What package?"

David picked up a small, square box. A note, addressed to Michaele Caraway, was tucked under the pink ribbon that bound it. "This one," he said.

"What is it?"

David shrugged. "How should I know?"

"Who's it from?"

"I don't know that either," David said. "I found it."

7 "HERE'S A MYSTERY for you, Sherlock," Michaele Caraway said to Sebastian a few minutes later. Holding the note before her, she read, " 'Love sought is good, but given unsought is better.' "

"That's all it says?" Sebastian asked. "What's it mean?"

"It's a quote from a play by Shakespeare called *Twelfth Night*. I think it's telling me I have a secret admirer."

"Any idea who it is?"

"None. You said you found it, David. Where?"

"It was under that big maple tree between the scenery shop and the theater."

"Under a tree. How romantic." Michaele shook her head and said "Well, perhaps you and your detective friend here can figure it out."

"Maybe what's in the box would give us a clue," David suggested. "Aren't you going to open it?"

"Absolutely," Michaele said, picking up the box and shaking it. "Something's moving around in there." Then, looking at Donovan, she asked, "This isn't from you, is it, angel?"

[26]

Donovan looked shyly at his mother. "I don't know Shakespeare," he said.

"Well, you never can tell." She turned to Sebastian and David and said, "Donovan and I are just getting to know each other." The two friends exchanged a look; it seemed an odd thing for a mother to say.

As Michaele picked at the ribbon with her long fingernails, Sebastian looked around the dressing room. It was pretty unimpressive, especially for a movie star. Its narrow width barely fit a makeup counter and chair on one side, daybed and table and lamp on the other. Most of the bulbs around the mirror's edge behind the makeup counter were burned out. The only illumination, other than what came from the few working bulbs, was provided by the little bit of sunlight that made its way through the grime-smeared window in the far wall. This room wasn't just unimpressive, Sebastian thought, it was downright bleak.

"I can't get it," Michaele said. Sebastian looked up. "There's a knot in this ribbon that won't budge."

"Maybe I can help," said David. "I'm good at knots." Taking the box from her, he set about his task. As he did, he began to whistle.

"David!" Michaele cried.

David looked up, startled. "What's the matter?"

"You're whistling in a dressing room."

David looked blankly at the actress. She seemed

serious, but he had no idea what she was talking about.

"It's bad luck, love. One must never whistle in a dressing room. I know it seems silly. But I believe in these old show business superstitions. Or perhaps I don't dare *not* to believe."

"I'm sorry," David said. "I hope I didn't jinx the show."

"I'm sure you didn't," Michaele said. "And there was no way you'd know. But in the future, no—"

"I know, no whistling. Do you still want help opening your present?"

"I'd love it."

A moment later, David lifted the lid of the box and looked inside. "I think it's a jar of nuts," he said.

"Is it?" Taking the box from David, Michaele removed the contents and held them up to view. "Macadamia nuts," she said. "My favorite. Now, I wonder who knew that."

Sebastian thought he heard someone outside. David must have heard it, too, because he said, "Maybe that's Rachel looking for me. I'd better get going."

"Yes," Michaele said. "I'm ready to go, too. It's awfully hot in here, isn't it?"

Sebastian said, "It's not so bad."

"It's me, then," said Michaele. "I'm feeling closed in. I don't like small rooms much."

"Maybe you should ask for a different dressing room," Sebastian said.

"No, I'll be all right as long as the door is always open. Just don't close me in, that's all I ask."

When Sebastian gave the actress a curious look, she explained, "When I was a little girl, I locked myself in a closet, and ever since, I've had this thing about small spaces. They terrify me." Suddenly, she laughed. "I must sound like the model of mental health. Superstitious, claustrophobic. I'm really not *so* bad. Still, what do you say we keep this conversation our little secret, shall we?"

Sebastian nodded. "All right," he said.

"Sure," said David, with a shrug. He didn't see what the big deal was, anyway. As they were about to leave, he cleared his throat and said, "Miss Caraway, I wanted to tell you that *Insectivore* is my very favorite movie. I thought you were great as the Spider Lady."

"Is he a friend of yours?" Michaele said to Sebastian.

Suddenly, she stopped short. A man was standing in the shadows of the hall. "There you are," the man said. "I've been looking all over for you."

"Oh, Dougie. You startled me."

"Sorry, love. I was wondering if you'd join me for dinner."

"Davey!" came a voice from the auditorium.

"I hate it when she calls me that," David mut-

[29]

tered. "I've gotta go. Bye, everybody. See you later, Sebastian." David ran off to find his sister.

"I'd love to join you for dinner," Michaele said to Dougie, "but I'm having dinner with Sebastian's family. I'm sorry, love."

"That's all right," Dougie said. "Maybe Doris and Rob are free. I'll see you tomorrow, then."

"Yes, tomorrow."

Turning to go, Dougie said, "God, I'm starved. I could eat a horse."

Michaele held out the jar she was carrying. "Would you settle for a nut?" she said.

"A nut? No, they don't agree with me."

"Don't they? I adore them. Especially macadamias. They're my favorite kind."

"I didn't know that," said Dougie.

"Someone does. Look." Michaele showed the director the card she had received.

"A secret admirer," he commented.

"That's just what I said." Squeezing his arm affectionately, Michaele said, "It isn't you, is it?"

Dougie Scott flushed slightly. "Of course not," he said. "My love for you is no secret."

Laughing, Michaele said, "You're such a lamb."

Dougie's cheeks were crimson.

8 THAT NIGHT after dinner, Sebastian sat with David on the front steps of his house. The two were deep in thought.

"The handwriting," David said at last.

"Hmm?"

"The handwriting on the note. That's one way to track down who Michaele's secret admirer is."

"I thought of that already. It's no good."

"Oh." David went back to thinking, then said, "What's wrong with it?"

"The note was written in some kind of fancy script, calligraphy or something, you know?" David nodded. "Anybody could do it, if he knew how. It's not like it's real handwriting."

"But all you have to do is find out who knows how to write like that."

Sebastian looked at his friend. "Obviously," he said, "whoever sent the note wants it to be a secret. He—or she—isn't going to let on that they know calligraphy."

"True. Well, maybe if you figured out who knew that quote from the Shakespeare play—"

"That wouldn't be very helpful. This is the theater. Everybody knows Shakespeare."

"Right. So what clues do we have to go on?"

"The macadamia nuts. If we knew where they were bought . . ."

David nodded thoughtfully. Then he said, "There's something else."

"What's that?"

"Whoever it is," said David, deliberately measuring his words, "*loves* Michaele Caraway."

"Oh, that's a big help," Sebastian said.

"No, wait, Sebastian. Maybe there'll be other signs to watch for. Does it seem like anybody in the cast loves her?"

"That's just the problem. *Everybody* loves Michaele Caraway."

"Everybody?"

"It seems like it. But I'll keep my eyes open anyway. We have a run-through of the play tomorrow morning, so the whole cast will be there."

Just then, Sebastian noticed someone coming up the sidewalk. He could hardly believe his eyes. It was Corrie. At least, he *thought* it was Corrie. She was wearing a dress and high heels.

"Don't laugh," she said, as she came closer.

"I'm not laughing," said Sebastian. "You look nice." David had his hand cupped over his mouth.

"Thank you," said Corrie.

"But why so dressed up?"

"To meet Michaele Caraway," said Corrie.

"Oh." Sebastian stood. "Come on in and meet her, then."

Corrie took a step toward the house. Her ankle turned under. "Stupid shoes," she muttered.

David shot a glance at Sebastian, and through his hand, "Is it okay to laugh now?"

9

" 'AND DO YOU THINK we'll be happier this time around?' " Michaele, as Heather Dexter, said.

" 'I know we'll be happy, darling,' " said Mark Lawson, as Jason Card. " 'We were just too young when we married the first time. Now that we've each been married and divorced twice, we have experience, we have wisdom, we have maturity—' "

" 'And we have five kids.' "

" 'Don't let a little thing like that worry you,' " Mark read. " 'You're forgetting—we also have five bathrooms!' "

" 'As Heather and Jason embrace, we hear the sound of five toilets flushing. And the curtain falls.' " Mintsy Jones read these last stage directions in her usual booming voice, then called out, "Very good run-through, everyone. Let's take a quick break, no more than five, then everybody back onstage for notes."

The actors scattered, some to the lobby for a drink of water, some outside to catch the late morning sun, some to the backstage area to talk and stretch and unwind. Sebastian was about to decline

[34]

Buster Wingate's whining request for a piggyback ride when Mark Lawson slapped him on the back and said, "Hey, big guy, what do you say we toss this Frisbee around?"

"Sorry," Sebastian said, picking up the five-year-old. "I'm busy."

Cliff Davies paced nervously up and down an aisle of the theater, jotting down notes on a spiral pad. Mintsy grabbed up some papers and ran out the side door of the auditorium. Only Dougie Scott did not move. His hands lay inertly on the sheet of ply-wood resting along the tops of the theater seats before him. The plywood served as a makeshift table for the director and stage manager, giving them a place to rest their scripts, their note pads, their styro-foam coffee cups. His eyes stared at the empty stage, seeming to see something that wasn't there.

"Boo!" said a voice from behind him.

Dougie didn't jump. He didn't even turn. "Michaele," he said softly.

"You're sitting here like the ghost at the banquet after the guests have gone."

"I'm just . . ."

Michaele came and sat by his side. Her hand reached out and touched his, gently. "Moved?" she said. "It is moving, isn't it? The mystery of breathing life into words. The magic. The theater."

Dougie Scott didn't say anything. He simply nodded.

"How did you think it went?" Michaele asked.

"How did *you?*"

"I was . . . well, surprised, to tell you the truth. It was so much better than I expected it to be. I really think it's going to work. No, more than that. I think it's going to be quite wonderful. Funny and touching and . . . do I dare say it, Dougie? I think we might even have a hit on our hands. Do you agree?"

"Oh," the director said. "Yes. That's just what I was thinking."

"I'm so glad, love," said Michaele.

"Onstage, everyone," Mintsy Jones called, as she reentered the auditorium. "Get out your pens and pencils. Time for notes."

"I don't have pens and pencils," said Buster Wingate, from atop Sebastian's shoulders.

"*You* may use a crayon," Mintsy said. She popped a chocolate mint into her mouth.

Buster wrapped his arms tightly around Sebastian's head. "Don't have a crayon either," he whispered.

"That may be true," said Sebastian, "but you've got one heck of a grip."

10

"NOTHING?" Corrie asked. The three friends were sitting under a big maple tree eating their lunch.

"Nothing," said Sebastian. "I mean, if we wanted evidence of how much everybody loves Michaele Caraway, I can give you plenty. Liz and Sarah Burke *both* came in wearing their hair like hers today. Rachel told me she's thinking of changing her name to Martine Castaway. Dougie Scott calls her 'love' and 'angel' all the time."

"But he calls everybody things like that," David interjected.

"True. But there's a *way* he says them to her. I can't describe it exactly. All I know is that he acts like the sun rises and sets on her, as Gram would say."

"What about Mark Lawson?"

"He keeps saying how great she is. When they're acting together, he tells her things like, 'That was a great moment, babe,' and 'Oh, wow, that was *so* real.' I can't tell whether he means that stuff or he's trying to impress her, but he seems to like her. Not at much as he likes himself, of course.

[37]

"As for Doris Carpenter and Rob McGrath, they keep to themselves a lot. But I did hear Doris saying to Rob how terrific Michaele was to work with, how she wasn't a prima donna like they'd expected. And Rob said that he was learning a lot about acting from her."

"So you're right," David said. "Everybody loves Michaele."

"Yep. Mintsy Jones asked her for her autograph today. And Cliff Davies . . . well, I'm not sure about him. But Michaele *did* say they were old friends."

"So her secret admirer could be anybody. Did you check out the macadamia nuts yet?"

"I haven't had a chance. But I will."

Just then, Mintsy Jones threw open the side door of the theater. "Two o'clock!" she shouted. "Let's go. Everybody onstage, pronto!"

Sebastian scrambled to his feet, wadding up his paper bag as he rose. "I left my script in my dressing room," he said. "See you guys later."

After Sebastian left, Corrie turned to David and said, "I can understand why everybody loves Michaele. After meeting her last night, I think I do too, a little."

"That's queer," said David.

"Not that way. I mean, she's special—and she makes *you* feel special too. You know?"

"That's because she's an actress," David said, rising. "Come on, let's get back to work."

[38]

11

SEBASTIAN HEARD VOICES coming from Michaele's dressing room. He stopped to listen.

"It's impossible," he heard Michaele say. "I know it's what you want, but it isn't what *I* want. Can't you see that?"

"But just give it a chance. Give *us* a chance," a man's voice said. The tone was hushed so Sebastian couldn't make out who the speaker was.

"Please," said Michaele. "I don't want to argue."

"How can you forget how good it was between us?"

"I'm not forgetting. But that was a long, long time ago. *You're* forgetting how bad things became."

All of a sudden, something clicked inside Sebastian's head. Michaele was practicing her lines with Mark Lawson. He couldn't remember the words exactly, but what he was overhearing did sound like that scene toward the end of the first act where Jason Card tries to win back his former wife by reminding her of the good times they'd shared. He had to laugh at himself; it was getting hard to tell illusion from reality around here. He stepped into his dressing room and picked up his script.

Turning to go, he heard something that made him stop and listen again.

"Can't we work together like two professionals?" Michaele was saying. "Must you drag in ancient history? Look, I want this production to be a success as much as you do. So, let's concentrate on that and not something that once was and can't be again. Cliff, are you listening?"

Sebastian got as close to his door as he could.

"I'm listening, Michaele," he heard Cliff say. "And what I hear is that you're as good at hurting me now as you ever were."

"Oh, Cliff."

A moment later, he heard the playwright and the actress walk down the hall toward the stage. Only when he was certain they had joined the others did he dare leave the room.

12

"WHERE ARE WE taking it from?" Sebastian heard Michaele ask as he walked onto the stage.

"Act One, Scene Three," Mintsy said. "Everybody but Michaele and Mark down front, please." The other actors moved off the stage to take seats in the front row of the auditorium.

"Now," said Mintsy, flipping the pages of her script. "Jason has just come in from the kitchen, carrying a wrench. Heather is standing by the front door. Mark, it'll be your line—'You're as nervous as—' "

"Got it," Mark called. Smiling at Michaele, he said, "You ready?"

"Ready as I'll ever be." Michaele seemed tight, distracted. Sebastian wondered if she was still thinking about Cliff.

He turned around to see the playwright hunched in his usual seat near the back of the auditorium. He was chewing on a fingernail, though, with more than customary vigor.

" 'You're as nervous as a mama cat,' " Mark read.

[41]

" 'With you here, it's hard not to be,' " said Michaele, as Heather.

" 'Why don't you sit down?' "

" 'I don't need to be invited to sit down in my own house.' "

" 'Then don't sit down.' "

" 'I'll sit if I want to,' " Michaele said. Looking up, she called out, "I cross to the sofa here, don't I, Mintsy?"

"That's right. You cross and sit."

Michaele walked slowly to the rehearsal sofa, which was not a sofa at all, but three old wooden chairs with delusions of upholstery. She sat on the one closest to the stage's edge. Without warning, the chair collapsed, crashing to the ground and bringing Michaele down with it.

"Ow!" she cried out sharply.

"Are you all right?" said Mark, throwing down his script and rushing to her side.

Dougie and Mintsy jumped out of their seats and hurried down the aisle. "Michaele, love, are you hurt?" Dougie cried.

Sebastian jumped up, too, glancing over his shoulder as he did. Cliff was staring at the stage. A concerned look was on his face, but he did not move.

"I'm all right, I'm all right," Michaele was saying, waving the others away. "At least, I think I am." Taking Mark's hand, she tried standing. "Oh," she

[42]

said, surprised at the pain she felt. "I think I've hurt my hip."

"Do you want to see a doctor?" Dougie asked.

"No, of course not, love. It isn't that serious. I'm sure I'll have nothing more to show for it than a bruise. The surprise was the worst of it." Dusting off her slacks, she said, "Let's go on, shall we? I'll be fine, really."

"You don't want a break?" said Dougie.

"No, I'm fine. I'm fine. Let's carry on, please."

"Mark," said Mintsy, "hand me that chair, will you? I'll give it to Richard to fix later. Grab another one from backstage for now."

A moment later, Mark returned with a new chair. He put it in place, then looked at Michaele and said, "You okay?"

Smiling weakly, Michaele nodded. "Shall we?"

Dougie and Mintsy had returned to their seats. Sebastian and the other kids were sitting. Michaele sat, gingerly, on the new old chair. And Mark said, " 'That's what I always loved about you, Heather—your independent mind.' "

" 'Don't condescend to me, Jason Card,' " said Michaele.

Sebastian turned around. Cliff Davies' seat was empty.

13

IT WAS LATER that afternoon.

"I can't say a line like that!" Mark Lawson said. "No, I take that back. I *can* say a line like that. But I *won't* say a line like that."

"Why not?" Cliff Davies shouted. He stormed down the aisle and grabbed hold of the stage's edge. His knuckles were fierce and white.

"Because it's stupid, that's why not. 'Darling, you're as soft as a baby's bottom and twice as sweet.' What kind of thing is that for a grown man to say to a woman?"

"I've told you before," Cliff said through gritted teeth. His eyes flared dangerously. "Jason Card is a poet."

"A true poet wouldn't be caught dead mouthing that kind of garbage," Mark shot back.

"And he's a father!" yelled the playwright.

"Well, if he's a father, he *knows* how sweet a baby's bottom is!"

"Boys!" Dougie Scott cried. He ran down the aisle and put a protective arm around Cliff's shoulder. Cliff shrugged it off.

[44]

"Who do you think you are?" Cliff said to Mark, his voice starting to shake. "The writer or something?"

"Funny," said Mark, "I was just going to ask you the same thing."

"I'm sorry I don't write the kind of verbal gems your writers provide you with on 'Love Is a Gas Attack,'" Cliff screamed.

Mark Lawson threw down his script. His hands tightened into fists as he advanced toward Cliff. Michaele, standing center stage, took a step in his direction, then stopped.

"'Love on the Fast Track' is *art* compared to this dribble," Mark shouted.

"The word is drivel, you ignoramus!"

"You'd know best what to call it! You wrote it!"

"Calm down, both of you," Dougie Scott said.

Cliff Davies said, "I will not calm down until this *actor* . . ." (He uttered the word as if referring to a disease-carrying rodent.) ". . . until this *actor* apologizes."

"*I* should apologize? You're the one who should apologize."

"Boys, boys!" said Dougie, mopping his brow.

Neither Cliff nor Mark heard. Their shouting only grew louder, their accusations angrier. All at once, Mintsy, whose voice had considerably more power than the director's, yelled "Cool it!"

Cliff and Mark stopped their shouting. All

[45]

heads turned in the direction of the stage manager, who smiled sweetly. "Shall we take a break?" she said. "And I think we'd better make it *ten* minutes this time."

14 SEBASTIAN WANDERED OFF by himself to the backstage area. He was checking out the system of dimmers and switches that controlled the stage lighting when he heard the back door of the theater open and close. A moment later, David appeared framed in the stage door.

"Hi," he said. "You on a break?"

Sebastian nodded.

"Us, too. I have something really important to tell you. You know that chair—" David stopped suddenly.

"Yeah? What about the chair?"

David shook his head. "Hi, Miss Caraway," he said. Sebastian turned and saw that Michaele was approaching.

"Please, David," she said, "call me Michaele. Well, Sebastian, what did you think of that little display?"

"I have concluded," Sebastian said, "that Mark has a temper."

"Yes, he certainly does. But he's right about

one thing, even if he doesn't know how to express it."

"What's that?"

"The play could stand improvement. Cliff always was difficult about rewrites. He's so sensitive. He thinks every word he writes is a nugget of gold. And everyone should value it as such. Words are more than words, of course. They are bridges from one person's soul to another. But they are not golden bridges. And if one support is shaky . . . well, then, it should be replaced. Better that than have the bridge fall apart. Yes?"

Sebastian nodded. "I see your point," he said.

David, a little confused, changed the subject. "How are you feeling, Miss Cara—Michaele?" he asked.

"Oh, since my little mishap, you mean? Better, thanks. I'm afraid I will have a nasty bruise. But I'm alive. There are worse things that can happen than having an old chair fall apart on you."

Sebastian said, "David was just going to tell me—"

"Donovan's doing okay," David said hastily.

"Pardon?" said Michaele.

"I just thought you might want to know how Donovan's doing. He's doing fine."

"Oh. Good."

There was the sound of running in the hall behind the stage. "Someone's in a hurry," said Michaele.

David turned around. "It sounded like somebody coming from your dressing room," he said.

"That's just what I was thinking," said Sebastian. "Let's take a look." He also thought, though he didn't mention it, that there was something unusual about the sound of those footsteps. He couldn't place it, but there was something . . . distinctive.

"Look," Sebastian said, as they approached the dressing room. He pointed through the open door. A box was sitting on the makeup counter.

"The mad masher strikes again," said Michaele.

"Huh?" David said.

"Never mind. Let's see what he left this time." Michaele took the box in hand, pulling the card out from under the ribbon. "It's a bigger box this time. Texas-size macadamia nuts, perhaps."

She read the card aloud. " 'If music be the food of love, play on.' *Twelfth Night* again. Well, you can't say he isn't consistent."

"Is it the same fancy writing?" Sebastian asked.

"Oh, yes," said Michaele. "Here, why don't you two hold onto the card? Perhaps it will help in your investigation."

The ribbon gave way easily this time. What Michaele found swathed in tissue paper was not a jar of macadamia nuts, after all, but a delicately carved music box. "Oh," she said, though the sound was more a breath than a word. "This is lovely."

She wound the key, and the tinkly music began

to play. "It's my favorite song," she said. "It's 'Greensleeves.' How did he know it was my favorite?" She paused and added, "Who is he?"

Just then, Rob McGrath appeared at the door. "There you are," he said. "They want to get started." Nodding toward the music box, he said, "Pretty. 'Greensleeves,' isn't it? Where'd you get it?"

"It's a gift," said Michaele. "A gift from a secret admirer. That wouldn't be you, would it, Rob?"

Rob broke into a big grin. "If it were, I'd never tell. There's too much pleasure in loving from afar. And none of the hassles."

Michaele laughed and put the music box down on the counter. "Very good, Rob McGrath," she said. "And too true, I'm afraid." She and Rob started down the hall.

"Wait a minute, Sebastian," David hissed, tugging at his friend's arm.

"I've got to get back to rehearsal."

"And I've got to get back to the shop. But this is important. It's about Michaele."

"What did I tell you?" said Sebastian. "Everybody loves her."

"Not everybody."

"What do you mean?"

"That chair didn't just fall apart by itself. Richard took a look at it. He said that one of the bolts was missing. Somebody removed it, Sebastian. Somebody wanted Michaele to get hurt."

15 THAT EVENING after dinner, Will
Barth asked Michaele if she'd like to
join the family in a game of Trivial
Pursuit.

"I've invited Josh Lepinsky over," Will told
her. "He's been dropping hints about meeting you.
I think you'll like him. He's got a great sense of
humor."

"I'm afraid he'll need one to be around me tonight," Michaele said. "I'm a bundle of nerves. And
not a very tightly tied one, at that."

Michaele, having moved with the others from
the kitchen to the sun-room, sat down on the wicker
love seat next to Sebastian's grandmother.

"You don't look the least bit nervous," Jessica
Hallem remarked, patting Michaele on the leg.

"I am, though. Everything went so well at yesterday's rehearsal. But today . . ."

"Today?" Katie said, prompting.

"Oh, I know it's silly. And I'm not blaming
your friend, Sebastian, but—"

"David?"

"Yes." Turning to the others, she said, "He

whistled in the dressing room yesterday."

"Bad luck, eh?" said Will Barth.

Michaele nodded slowly. "I wouldn't have thought anything of it, but this afternoon so much went wrong. There was the accident with the chair I told you about. And Mark Lawson, the leading man, had a terrible fight with Cliff. They made up later, but it put an awful damper on things. Mark has an explosive temper, and Cliff . . . well, Cliff can be . . . difficult." Michaele looked away. After a moment, she said, "This friend of yours, what does he do?"

"Josh?" said Katie. "He's a writer."

"A writer!" Michaele said, with a little laugh. "Not a writer!"

"What do you mean, dear?" asked Jessica.

"Nothing," Michaele said. "It's just—oh, why am I being so secretive? It's not such a big deal. Cliff, the author of this little play of ours, is an old beau."

"An old what?" Sebastian asked.

"That's what we used to call boyfriends," Jessica said. "Long before your time, dear. Long before Michaele's, for that matter."

"Oh." Sebastian averted his eyes. He didn't want Michaele to know that he had overheard her conversation with Cliff.

"An old boyfriend, then," said Michaele. "We met when I was cast in an off-Broadway production of a play of his. This was right out of college. It was, as they say in the storybooks, love at first sight. But the romance, like the play, was short-lived. The reviews closed the play in three days, and on the fourth I left Cliff a note, telling him good-bye. I'm afraid he took it very badly. Even threatened to kill himself, the poor lamb. He began to phone me constantly. I was forced to get an unlisted number. I felt terrible, but what could I do?"

Katie nodded sympathetically.

Michaele sighed and tucked her legs under her. "I guess one of the reasons I'm doing this play is guilt. It was rotten of me to leave Cliff when he was down like that. I should have waited at least until he was feeling better."

"Why didn't you?" Will asked.

Michaele sighed again. "He was so hard to be around. Sulky, demanding, childish. That's Cliff, I'm afraid. He's still a baby, really. After I left him, I was in a hit on Broadway, then went to Hollywood. My career soared upward, while Cliff's trudged along the flat and even course of mediocrity. So there was something else to feel guilty about. Of course, guilt isn't the only reason I'm here. It *is* a good play and it's a good part for me. And somewhere, deep down inside, I still care for Cliff—as a friend. The problem is that he wants more. He wants to go back to something that once was, even if it was something that was mostly in his imagination."

There was a long moment of silence. One of

Sebastian's cats, the one missing a tail, sauntered into the room and surveyed its occupants with a superior gaze.

"Come here, Chopped Liver," Sebastian called softly. The cat eyed Sebastian suspiciously, as if unsure whether the boy on the pillow were his master or some imposter. He crossed the room and, when a few sniffs had convinced him this was the real Sebastian Barth, curled up and began to purr loudly.

"Well," said Jessica Hallem at last, "I do hope things go better for you tomorrow."

Michaele laughed. "Things are going splendidly," she said. "I'm just being melodramatic. I'm afraid that bit of whistling in the dressing room set off a little stage fright in me. All of a sudden, all my little insecurities poked their way out of the places I'd neatly tucked them and began running rampant. How do I dare complain? I'm on the stage again, in the company of wonderful, caring people. One can feel the love in the air. *And* let's not forget that I have a secret admirer."

Sebastian thought of the chair and of the bolt that had been deliberately removed.

"Besides, how much of a curse can a little whistling bring?" Michaele went on. "Today's rehearsal is over. Let's hope that's the end of the bad luck."

"I'm sure it is," said Jessica.

Josh Lepinsky appeared at the door. "I let myself in," he said.

[54]

Everyone laughed.

"What's so funny?" he asked. "Is something stuck between my teeth?"

"No, no," said Katie, getting up and taking Josh's arm. "We were just speculating on the possibility of more bad luck coming Michaele's way when you arrived."

"Well," said Josh, "you can't say I don't know how to time an entrance."

"Michaele, this is our dearest friend, Josh Lepinsky. Josh, Michaele Caraway."

Josh took Michaele's hand and held it gently. "A pleasure," he said, looking into her eyes. "And I want you to know that as long as you are in Pembroke, I will personally guarantee that no bad luck comes your way."

A loud crash came from the direction of the kitchen.

"You're fired," Michaele said with a startled laugh, as she and Katie ran from the room. Josh looked at the others with chagrin.

"Don't worry," Sebastian told him. "That wasn't bad luck. That was Donovan."

16

THE NEXT MORNING, Sebastian and David were sitting on the front steps of David's house, waiting for Michaele to drive them to the theater. "What did Josh have to say when he got home last night?" Sebastian asked.

"I don't know. I was in bed already. But I heard him singing some dippy love song when he was coming up the stairs."

"Oh-oh," said Sebastian.

"Yeah. And this morning he poured orange juice on his cereal."

"Sounds like he's been bitten."

David nodded. "It's a good thing we're immune to that sort of thing, right, Sebastian?"

Sebastian didn't answer. Instead, he said, "By the way, I found out Donovan's story last night."

"What do you mean?"

"Remember when Michaele said she and Donovan were just getting to know each other?"

"Yeah."

"Well, it seems that Michaele was married to

[56]

this guy named Frank. When Donovan was six, she and Frank split up. They asked Donovan who he wanted to live with and—"

"Modern parents," said David.

"And he chose his father. So for the last three years, Donovan's been living with Frank in New York while Michaele's been making movies in California. I guess things weren't going so well, because they decided about a month ago that Donovan should live with Michaele."

"That's all the time they've been together?"

"Other than a week or two here and there over the years."

"Wow. No wonder they don't know each other."

Just then, they saw the front door of Sebastian's house open, and through it came Michaele and Donovan. Donovan's hands were stuffed in his pockets. His mother reached out to touch him, and he pulled away.

"He's in a good mood," David said.

"As usual. Listen, we should get going if we're going to ride with Michaele. Where's Rachel?"

"I'll get her." Pulling open the screen door, David called, "Twerp! Let's go!" Coming back to Sebastian, he said, "Do you have any idea who pulled that trick with the chair?"

"I have a hunch," said Sebastian. "I think it's her secret admirer."

"But why would somebody who's sending her love notes want to hurt her? That doesn't make sense."

"I know it doesn't. But it just might. I have a few things to check up on before I'm sure."

"Such as?"

"Did anybody move that chair right before rehearsal yesterday? If they did, I have a pretty good idea who it was . . . and why."

"And then you'll know who the secret admirer is, too?" David asked. "Who do you think it is?"

Sebastian watched Donovan run from his mother to the car. Michaele stayed behind, shaking her head. Turning to David, he said, "Let's just say I have a hunch."

Rachel burst out of the house. "Am I late?" she said. "I was practicing my faces in the mirror."

"You're not supposed to make faces, Rachel," said Sebastian. "You're supposed to act."

"How can you act without making faces?" Rachel said. "You have a lot to learn yet, Sebastian. Hey, David told me that you're interviewing Michaele and Mark and Dougie on your radio show this afternoon, and I want to know why you're not interviewing me. I have an important part in this play, you know."

"For starters, you're not famous," Sebastian said.

"Not yet, maybe. But one day the name Sondra Sage will be as well known as . . . as . . ."

"Ty-D-Bol?" said David.

"What happened to Martine Castaway?" Sebastian asked.

"It seemed . . . used, somehow. Anyway, I like Sondra Sage better. It's more *me*." Spotting Michaele across the street, Rachel ran toward her, waving her arms. "Michaele, Michaele!" she cried. "Are you going to marry my father?"

David dropped his head into his hands.

17

"NO," MINTSY SAID to Sebastian, "I didn't see anybody touch it. Everything was just where we left it after the morning rehearsal."

"And you're sure it was the same chair?" Sebastian asked.

"Positive. Listen, Sebastian, Richard and I had a long talk about it last night. The only time somebody could have messed with that chair was during lunch. Once people started coming back in for rehearsal, no one went near it."

"During lunch," Sebastian said, as Mintsy turned away to talk to Mark Lawson. "So it wasn't him. Unless—"

"Talking to yourself, eh?" Sebastian felt a hand on his shoulder. He turned to see Dougie Scott smiling at him. "Has the pressure gotten to be too much for you?"

"Just practicing my lines," said Sebastian.

"Good for you. They have to be learned by tomorrow, you know."

"I know."

"I'm looking forward to being on your program

this afternoon, Sebastian. What's it called again?"

" 'Small Talk'."

"Yes, well, I'm looking forward to it." The director looked toward the stage, now dominated by a giant structure of two-by-fours. "Isn't it lucky the theater is dark this week?" he said.

"Dark?" said Sebastian.

"That's a theater term. It means there's no play being performed right now. We have the place all to ourselves. We'd never have the set on stage so soon otherwise. What do you think of it, by the way?"

"It sort of looks like the dinosaur at the Museum of Natural History."

"An apt analogy," said Dougie. "The bones are there, but not the flesh. The flesh will come soon enough. Unfortunately, we will be hampered this morning by a lack of stairs. They're to be put in during the lunch break. But, this afternoon, we shall have the full use of . . . ah, Michaele."

"Good morning, love," said Michaele, kissing Dougie's cheek. "How are you today?"

"Well, thank you. The question is, how are *you*? How's the bruise?"

"It hurts. But I'm feeling rested. A good night's sleep is always the best cure."

" 'Sleep that knits up the ravelled sleave of care,' " Mark said, joining them. He sipped at a thermos cup of coffee.

"That's from something," Michaele said.

[61]

"One of the great roles of my college career."

"It's from *Macbeth*," said Dougie Scott.

"Dougie!" Michaele cried.

Dougie put a hand to his mouth. "I said it!"

"Said what?" said Sebastian.

"One is never supposed to mention that play by name," Dougie said. "It's terribly bad luck in the theater. One must refer to it only as 'the Scottish play.' "

Michaele had grown pale. "Yes," she said. "It's the worst bit of bad luck. There are stories, dozens of them, hundreds, of bad luck coming to a production where the Scottish play has been mentioned. *Or*," she said, turning to Mark, "where one of its lines have been quoted."

Mark said, "I'm sorry, Michaele. I didn't know. I work in TV, remember?"

Dougie reached out and took Michaele's hands in his. "Will you forgive me, my angel?" he said. "It was thoughtless and foolish of me to blurt out the name like that. I know how much you believe in these superstitions. Look how upset you were about that young fellow whistling in your dressing room."

"I wasn't *that* upset," said Michaele. "Still, bad luck did follow. And whistling in the dressing room is nothing compared to the Scottish play. Oh, Dougie."

"My dear," said Dougie Scott, "you mustn't take it so to heart. After all, if the Scottish play were such a terrible curse, there wouldn't be a production of it done anywhere, would there? And it's performed frequently."

"That's true enough," Michaele said. The color was returning to her face. "Tell me I'm being a silly goose and let's get on with it."

"You're being a silly goose," said Dougie, dutifully.

"Places for Act Two," Mintsy shouted.

18

"TIP IT UP. That's it, Steve, your end. Sebastian—that's your name, isn't it?—grab hold there by David. There we go, lads. We've got it now."

"You're a chauvinist," Corrie said to the technical director, once the first piece of the staircase had been maneuvered through the auditorium door. "I could have helped. I have muscles, too, you know."

"I'm sure you do, lovely," Richard said, "but, well . . ."

"Ha!" said Corrie. "You can't think of an excuse, can you?"

"All right, the next bit is all yours."

Sebastian, who had volunteered to help the crew load the stairs onto the stage during his lunch break, couldn't help noticing that Richard spoke with the same English accent as Sally, the costume lady. "Are they friends or something?" he asked David, as they knelt to hammer the structure into place.

"I think so," David said. "They act like they are."

"Splendid," Sebastian heard Richard say. He

looked up. "You're doing a splendid job, lads. I appreciate your help, Sebastian. We're a few people short today. I think I worked them a little hard last night getting this monstrosity up. Ah, here comes the rest of the stairs."

Richard walked to the lip of the stage and guided the struggling stair-carriers (all female) down the side aisle. Sebastian smiled to see the look of determination in Corrie's eyes.

He liked Richard and told David so. David nodded. "He's kind of shy and quiet. But he's a nice bloke."

Sebastian gave David a look.

"That's how he'd say it," David said.

As the workers finished attaching the staircase to the stage floor and the rest of the set, the side door of the auditorium opened. Michaele Caraway stood half in sunlight, half in shadow.

"There you are, Sebastian," she said. "We were looking for you. We're running lines from Act One. Do you want to join us?"

"Sure," Sebastian said. "That is . . ." He looked at Richard.

"Well done, lad," he said. "Off with you. And thanks."

"See you later, David," Sebastian said. "So long, Corrie." He jumped down from the stage and grabbed his brown-bag lunch from a seat in the first row.

"The set looks wonderful, Richard," Michaele called out. "It's beginning to feel like home."

"Thank you, ma'am," Richard said. His reverential tone made Sebastian turn and look up. Richard's head was bowed, as if he were in a church.

19 AFTER EATING his lunch and running lines with the rest of the cast, Sebastian walked with Michaele to her dressing room.

On the makeup counter was a bouquet of yellow roses. And leaning beside the vase that held them was a note, written in the same calligraphic hand as the others.

> *Doubt thou the stars are fire;*
> *Doubt that the sun doth move;*
> *Doubt truth to be a liar;*
> *But never doubt I love.*

"*Hamlet* this time," said Michaele, touching a rose with a gentle, tentative hand. "He's getting serious."

20 WHEN THEY RETURNED to the stage, the theater was empty. The crew had finished their work; the cast had not yet assembled for the afternoon rehearsal.

"No one here but the ghosts," Michaele commented. "I do love the ghosts."

Within moments, however, the ghosts were displaced by a boisterous bunch of actors, eager to get to work.

Mark and Rob were asked to report to the costume shop for fittings while the other actors were encouraged to walk around the stage now that the stairs had been put in place.

"Just to get the feel of the whole set," Mintsy said.

"But as there are no railings yet," said Dougie, "I'd rather you go up the stairs one at a time. For safety's sake." Michaele, who was on the stage already, volunteered to go first.

It happened suddenly. Too suddenly to shout out a warning. Too suddenly to stop it. As she reached the fourth stair, Michaele's foot skidded, almost comically, across the wood. Her hands flew up, her leg out and, before she knew what had happened, she was lying on the stage floor, her legs twisted beneath her. The others came running.

"Oh my god," Dougie Scott said, as he knelt by her. "Are you all right, Michaele? Speak to me, dear girl."

"Don't be so melodramatic, love," said Michaele. She winced as she tried to sit up. "I'm not dead. Though I might feel better if I were."

"Are you in much pain?" Cliff asked.

"Enough," she said. "Enough."

Mintsy Jones shook her head. "Why aren't Rob and Mark here? Cliff, see if you and . . . and . . ." She looked around her. "Sebastian, do you think you can help Cliff get Michaele on her feet? Let's get her to a doctor, pronto."

Sebastian and Cliff took Michaele's arms around their shoulders and lifted. Sebastian noticed the tears frozen on Michaele's cheeks. She didn't utter a sound until she tried to put both feet down. Then she cried out sharply.

"It's the right one," she said. "I think it's . . . I don't know . . . I think it's broken or something."

"Good god," Dougie sputtered. "This is terrible. Something must be done. Mintsy, get Richard in here. I want an explanation."

[69]

"There's a simple explanation, Dougie," Michaele said. She paused for effect. "It's the curse of the Scottish play."

Dougie's face fell. "Don't say that," he said. "If it's true, then I'm to blame."

"Of course you're not," said Michaele. "If anyone's to blame, it's Shakespeare. He wrote the thing, after all."

THE DOCTOR diagnosed Michaele's injury as a bad sprain. At least it wasn't a break, she said. That was true, he replied, but a sprain was not to be taken lightly. He taped her ankle and told her she'd have to use crutches. If possible, he said, she should keep off her foot for the next few days.

"It isn't possible," Michaele told Dougie, leaving the doctor's office. Sebastian and Cliff followed behind.

"You must think of your health," the director said.

"What about the health of the play?" said Michaele.

"We could . . . we could get an understudy," Dougie suggested.

"An understudy! Dougie, how could you say such a thing? No, no understudy. I can rehearse on crutches. I'll be fine by opening night."

"But, Michaele, what if these things keep happening?"

[70]

Michaele stopped walking and looked into the director's eyes. "What do you mean?" she asked.

"I . . . Perhaps I was a fool to mention the Scottish play, but I may be an even bigger fool to discredit the notion of its curse."

"Do you mean that you believe in the curse?"

"I don't know what to believe anymore," said Dougie. "I'm worried, that's all."

"I can see it in your face," Michaele said, "and I appreciate your concern. But we mustn't let a few mishaps make us crazy. We still have Cliff's wonderful play."

Turning to Cliff, she said, "It is wonderful, you know."

Cliff looked a little sadly at Michaele and said, "Only because you're in it."

Michaele cocked her head. "Nonsense," she said. "What makes you say these things, Cliff?"

REHEARSALS continued that afternoon as best they could under the circumstances. Michaele got around in an antique wheelchair someone had found in the prop room. "I'm staying off my feet," she called out to the director. "Just as the doctor ordered."

During a break, Sebastian overheard Mintsy and Dougie talking.

"I can't believe it," Dougie was saying. "Are you sure?"

"Absolutely," Mintsy Jones said. "There was grease on the step."

"Grease?"

Mintsy nodded. "And Richard said that no grease was used in putting the stairs up. He checked them himself before he left. There was no grease on them then. And he was the last to leave."

"What do you make of it?"

"I hate to say it, Dougie, but after that incident with the chair, it looks as if somebody is out to get Michaele or maybe to stop the play. That grease didn't get there by itself, you know. Somebody wanted to make sure that somebody fell."

Dougie looked around the room. His eyes caught Sebastian's before he turned back to the stage manager and said, "But who would be so cruel, Mintsy? That's what I don't understand."

Mintsy did not have an answer. Sebastian didn't either. But later that afternoon when the entire company was assembled for notes, he looked at each face in turn. And wondered.

21 AFTER REHEARSAL, Sebastian and David rode with Dougie and Mark to WEB-FM, the radio station where each Wednesday Sebastian taped his program, "Small Talk." David was the writer for the show.

"I'd been so looking forward to this, Sebastian," the director said, glancing in his rearview mirror at the boys. "It's been a long time since I was interviewed. But now with what's happened to Michaele, I don't know, I . . . feel distracted. It's a shame Michaele can't do the show. You do understand, don't you?"

"Sure," Sebastian said. "I'm just glad you were still willing to do it."

"Of course we are," said Dougie. "We're a couple of troupers, aren't we, Mark? 'The show must go on' and all that sort of thing."

"Really." Mark turned to face Sebastian. "Tell me, big guy," he said. "This show . . . it's for kids, right?"

"Mostly," Sebastian said.

"Well, what should we talk about? I mean, I'm

out of touch with kids, you know. I'm into being an adult."

You could have fooled me, Sebastian thought.

"Yes," Dougie said. "What sorts of things will you be asking?"

Sebastian turned to David who looked up from his note pad. "I figured Sebastian would ask you questions about the play," he said. "I've got fifteen so far. Do you want to hear them?"

"Just about the play?" Dougie said. "Don't you want to know about me?"

"Well . . . uh, sure."

"I have some wonderful stories about my early career that'll amuse your young listeners. There was the time I was stranded with a touring company of *Naughty Marietta* in a barn in Iowa. This was a long time ago—in the forties, I think. I was an actor then. Anyway, a storm was coming up and—"

"I was thinking I could talk about 'Love on the Fast Track,'" said Mark, seeming not to have noticed that Dougie was speaking. "I'll bet a lot of your listeners watch my show. I mean, it *is* the number one rated soap. I'm not just saying that; it's a fact. And I *was* voted the 'Man I'd Most Like to Be Stuck in a Stalled Elevator With' by the readers of *Seventeen*. Hey, here's a funny story . . ."

Sebastian and David exchanged a look, as David quietly tore up his list of questions.

[74]

AFTER THE half-hour program had been taped and Dougie and Mark had departed, Sebastian and David collapsed against the hard plastic surfaces of the furniture in the station's reception area.

"I don't believe it," David said. "That was the worst show we ever did."

"Dougie is such a nice guy I didn't have the heart to stop him from telling all those stories," said Sebastian.

"And you couldn't have stopped Mark if you'd wanted to. Hey, big guy, do you believe how much he had to say about his boots?"

"What about Dougie's story about the time he forgot his lines and just walked off the stage?"

"And Mark talking about his tap dance lessons when he was ten."

Something clicked in Sebastian's head. Something about the sound of those shoes he'd heard in the hall outside Michaele's dressing room. He pushed the thought aside for the moment. "And those imitations Dougie did of Bela Lugosi and Jimmy Cagney and Lionel Barrymore. Who are those guys, anyway?"

"Bela Lugosi was the original film Dracula," said Sebastian's father, entering the room. Will Barth was WEB's station manager. "Jimmy Cagney was best known for his gangster roles, though he got his start as a song-and-dance man. And Lionel Barrymore was one of the famous Barrymores, a family of great actors."

"Oh," said Sebastian. "Well, the point is that he did all these impersonations of people nobody normal has ever heard of."

Will shook his head. "Was he good at least?"

"How do I know?" said Sebastian. "I asked him to do Michael Jackson. That stumped him."

"Did he talk about the play much?"

"Not really," David said. "Every time Sebastian asked him about it, he'd *start* to talk about it. Then he'd remember something that happened to him a billion years ago, and he was gone."

"I feel sorry for him," Sebastian said. "It's like he lives in the past. If this play isn't a hit, I don't know what he'll do."

"Mark wasn't quite as bad," David told Will. "He talked about the play a little."

"Yeah," said Sebastian, "*his* part in it."

"It sounds like you two need a break," said Will. "Why don't you go out and throw a ball around?"

"Can't," Sebastian said. "We have some other stuff to do. And tonight I have to learn the rest of my lines."

"Oh, well," Will said. "You know what they say."

"What's that?"

" 'There's no business like show business.' "

"Hmm," said Sebastian, stroking his chin. "That's catchy. Put it to music, and you might have something."

22 FROM THE RADIO STATION, Sebastian and David walked to Main Street, stopping at a gourmet food shop called "Exotic Eats." Sebastian found the display he was looking for on the wall to the right of the door as they entered. The small jars of macadamia nuts were identical to the one Michaele had received. As he picked a jar off the shelf to examine it more closely, a woman said from behind him, "Are you looking for something in particular?"

The boys turned. The woman was giving them that look salespeople sometimes give kids, the one that says, "Don't think I don't know what you're up to." Why did some people assume that all kids were shoplifters? Guilty until proven innocent, Sebastian thought.

"I was wondering about these macadamia nuts," he said.

"They're expensive," said the woman.

"I know. I read the price. What I was wondering—"

"Yes?"

[78]

"I was wondering if these nuts were sold some-place else?"

The saleswoman arched her eyebrows. "If you're hoping to underprice us, I'm afraid you'll have no luck," she said. "We are the only store in the area that carries this brand. Would you like to buy a jar?"

"Well, to tell you the truth," Sebastian said, "no." The woman's eyebrows dropped. "But maybe you can help me, anyway. Somebody gave me a jar of these for my birthday a few days ago, but I can't find the card that went with them. I was hoping maybe you'd remember who bought them, so I could send a thank-you note. I feel bad because whoever it was spent a lot of money."

"Many people shop here," said the saleswoman. "I can't hope to remember everyone. Sorry." She lifted the jar from his hands and gave him a smile that was anything but friendly.

"Well, I guess we'll be going," Sebastian said. The woman nodded. As he and David moved toward the door, Sebastian said, "Do you get the feeling we're tracking mud all over their nice carpets or something?"

"Yeah," David said. He couldn't help checking the floor behind him as he went.

They fared no better at the music store. "The music box you describe," the salesman told them,

[79]

"doesn't sound like one of ours. It's rather more elaborate than the type we sell. I suspect it was purchased in Hartford or New York. There's no other store around here that would carry it, I'm sure of that."

"Hartford or New York?" David said, as they left. "We can't check every music store on the East Coast, Sebastian."

"I know," said Sebastian. "But we still have the flower shop."

"A dozen yellow roses," the florist said. "Yes, of course I remember selling a dozen yellow roses today."

Sebastian and David looked at each other with hope.

"But I couldn't tell you who I sold them to. It was a cash transaction. You say they were sent to your mother and there was no card attached?"

Sebastian nodded.

The florist shrugged. "Maybe the giver wished to be anonymous. Have you asked your father?"

"I'm sure they're not from my father," Sebastian said. "That's just the problem, you see. If I don't find out who it is, it could . . ." He dropped his head. "It could mean trouble for my parents' marriage."

"Oh, my. You *do* have a problem, don't you?"

"Could you describe the person who bought them?" David asked.

"A tall fellow. Young. Not as young as you, but . . ."

"How old would you say?"

"Sixteen, seventeen. I didn't take a careful look. He knew what he wanted, came and left. And I had other customers at the time. But I do remember one thing."

"What's that?" asked Sebastian.

"He had red hair."

"Red hair? Are you sure?"

Oh, yes, I'm positive about that. He had a nice head of red hair." The phone rang. "If you'll excuse me," said the florist.

"*Nobody* has red hair," David said outside. "Nobody but Corrie, and she isn't sixteen."

"Or a boy. So maybe it isn't somebody from the theater, after all."

"You mean it could be an outsider?" David asked.

"It could be," said Sebastian. "We'd better be on the lookout."

"Wanted," David said. "One suspicious-looking redhead."

23 DONOVAN DIDN'T SAY a word all during dinner.

"You're quieter than usual to-night," Katie said at last. "Is something wrong?"

The boy just shook his head.

"Are you feeling all right, love?" Michaele asked.

He nodded indifferently.

The others at the table exchanged worried looks. Then Jessica said, "Donovan may have troubles known to him alone. When he wishes to share them, he will. Tell me, Will, what did you think of the President's remarks on the economy today?"

After dinner, Michaele asked Donovan to join her on the front porch. "I think we should have a little talk," she said to him.

Fifteen minutes later, the front door flew open and slammed shut. Sebastian, who was sitting in the living room, looked up from his script to see Donovan run by and up the stairs. He walked to the front door and looked out. Michaele, leaning on her crutches, was staring up at the pale moon in the still blue sky.

Hearing Sebastian at the door, she turned. "It's like a ghost," she said, nodding toward the moon. "It's there but isn't."

"Do you want to be alone?" Sebastian asked.

"No. Come out. Keep me company."

Sebastian stepped out onto the porch. Michaele smiled, a little sadly. "Why can't I have a son like you?" she said.

"What?"

She looked away then. "I'm sorry," she said. "That was a foolish thing to say. It's just . . . it's just that it seems we always want what we can't have. And what we have, we don't want. My father wanted a son. He didn't have one, so he gave me a boy's name. Michael-with-an-e. Mike, he called me sometimes. I was his favorite. And he was mine. I wanted him to live forever. But I didn't get what I wanted, you see. He died when I was twelve."

"I'm sorry," Sebastian said.

"When Donovan was born, I wanted to give him the world. But I managed instead to mess up the already imperfect world he was born into. I wanted him to be bright and talented and special and . . . and he's sulky and difficult and quite, quite ordinary."

Michaele crossed slowly to the porch swing and sat down. Sebastian sat by her side. "Sometimes Donovan wants a different mother, sometimes I want a different son. Cliff wants to love me. I want to be

[83]

loved. But not by Cliff. Complicated, isn't it?"

Sebastian didn't know what to say. He just listened. And tried to understand.

"I'll tell you something I haven't told a soul," Michaele said then. "I joke about it, but I really am frightened."

"Frightened of what?" Sebastian asked.

"Of acting on the stage again. Of finding out that I can't. Of being a failure."

"But you're a famous actress. You know you can act."

"Being a famous actress isn't necessarily the same as being a good one. I know that I can act in the movies. But that isn't the same as acting on the stage. That . . . that going out there every night, being *seen*, taking chances . . . it all takes such courage. I thought I had it, but now I don't know. These . . . things . . . that have been happening, they've shaken the little confidence I had. I'm not sure how I feel about this secret admirer of mine. At first, I thought it was charming. But now, I don't know. It worries me, somehow."

"I'll find out who it is," Sebastian said. "At least, I'll try."

"I know you will," said Michaele. She reached across the swing and touched Sebastian's hand lightly. "You're very sweet. If only . . ."

"If only what?"

Michaele pulled her hand away. "Nothing,"

she said. She was silent a moment, then said, "This business with Donovan. I don't need it. I don't need it now."

Sebastian said nothing. Inside, the telephone was ringing.

"Don't you want to get to work on your lines?" Michaele asked.

Sebastian nodded. "I'll go in in a minute," he said.

"You know, you're doing wonderfully in the play, Sebastian. You have the makings of a real actor."

"Really?"

"Oh, yes. I can tell. There's a way you—"

The front door opened. Katie popped her head out and said, "Michaele, telephone for you. It's Dougie. Is Donovan all right?"

Michaele, still getting used to her crutches, rose slowly. "I don't know what his problem is. He won't tell me." Then she said, "I've been having a real grown-up conversation with your son. He's very special, Katie. I hope you appreciate that."

Katie was surprised at Michaele's remark. "Oh, I do," she said.

"You get going on those lines now, you hear?" said Michaele to Sebastian.

"I will," Sebastian said.

"And thanks for listening." Sebastian just smiled as Michaele disappeared into the house with Katie.

[85]

He tried to make sense of all that she had said to him. He knew only two things for certain: she was troubled, and she had confided her deepest fears to no one but him. To him. He had to find out who was trying to hurt her. He had to save her and give her back the confidence she needed.

Looking up at the darkening sky, he wondered if he would be a real actor one day. A real actor, perhaps, who would appear in a play or a movie with Michaele Caraway. Not as her son, but as the younger man she loves. He felt very warm suddenly. Rising, he decided to go up to his room and study his lines. He'd put the fan on.

He took one last look at the moon. It was no longer a ghost. In fact, to him, it appeared almost as radiant as the sun.

24

THE NEXT DAY, Donovan disappeared.

It happened sometime in the early afternoon. Richard interrupted the rehearsal to let Michaele know her son was gone. An hour's search by everyone in the company failed to turn up any evidence of where he'd been or where he'd gone.

Only Sebastian found something.

It was a card, leaning against the vase of roses in Michaele's dressing room. It was written in the same style as the others, and it read:

Parting is such sweet sorrow.

25

IT WAS SEVEN O'CLOCK.
Michaele stood in the entrance-
way to the kitchen, staring down the
hall to the front door of the house. "I can't eat a
thing," she said, feeling Katie's hand touch her
shoulder.

"I'm sure he's all right," Katie said. "He'll come
back soon."

Michaele turned and looked into the eyes of her
old friend. "I hope you're right," she said. "Please
be right."

Sitting at the table, Sebastian and his father exchanged worried glances. His grandmother busied
herself arranging the hastily purchased cold cuts and
assorted salads that were to serve as dinner on this
out-of-joint evening. Stirring cups of reheated coffee
were Dougie and Sally, who had helped Michaele
continue to search for Donovan that afternoon and
accompanied her home that evening. Everyone was
awaiting the arrival of Police Chief Alex Theopoulos.

"We pay the police in this town handsomely
enough," Jessica Hallem had said an hour earlier.
"Let them earn their money."

At the sound of the front door opening, Michaele called out her son's name. Seeing that it was only Josh and David, she began to cry. Accompanying Josh and his son was a tall, burly man wearing a pink knit shirt.

"No word?" Josh asked. When Michaele shook her head, he said, "This is Alex Theopoulos. He's the police chief here. And a good friend, Michaele. He'll help."

"Coffee, Josh? Alex?" said Katie.

Both men declined. Alex's large hand reached out to encompass Michaele's, which was trembling. "I'm sorry," he said to her. "I'll do what I can. The police shouldn't really be called in on a case like this until twenty-four hours have passed. So let's say I'm here because I'm concerned, unofficially and personally."

"Thank you," Michaele said, pulling in her tears.

"Let's start from the beginning," Alex said. "David, why don't you tell everybody what you told me at your house just now?"

David said, "I was the first one to notice that Donovan was missing, I guess. It was about eleven o'clock. I thought maybe he hadn't come in. Then I remembered seeing him when we'd first gotten there . . ."

"Which was when?"

"Around ten. Anyway, I told Richard, and he

[89]

said that he'd show up sooner or later and I shouldn't worry. When it was time for lunch, about one-thirty, I told Richard that Donovan was still missing. This time, he got worried. He asked us—you know, the apprentices—if we'd seen him. Nobody had."

Alex pulled at his chin. "Did you notice anything else, David? Was there anything different about anyone today? Was anyone absent? Did anyone leave for a long period of time?"

David thought for a moment, then shook his head. "Everybody was there who usually is. And working hard. I didn't see anybody leave. Of course, I was working hard, too. So someone could have left without my seeing it, I guess."

"What about the apprentices? Who are they?"

Sally spoke up. "They're all local kids," she said. "Some have been with us for the whole summer. Some, like David, just came on for this show. They're all good, reliable kids."

"What about this Richard, is that his name?"

"Funny story, that," said Sally. "We lost our regular technical director a few weeks ago. Seems he got an offer elsewhere that he couldn't refuse. Of course, we were in a panic. Then Richard phoned me up, just to say hello. He's an old, dear friend—and a very good technical director. Well, I offered him the job. Just like that. I didn't really think he'd take it. He's big time now, you see. But he said he'd enjoy the chance to get away from New York for a few weeks. So here he is."

"What about the regular technical director, the one who left? What was he like?"

Sally didn't answer right away. "An odd duck, he was. I don't mean to speak ill of him, but he was . . . a bit eccentric. Kept to himself most of the time. He was competent, don't get me wrong. He just wasn't the most outgoing person in the world."

"But then," said Dougie Scott, "neither is Richard."

"That's true," said Sally. "He's dreadfully shy. But he's a love." She almost blushed when she said it.

"The former technical director," said Alex, "what was his name?"

"Brian Butterworth."

"Where did this new job take him?"

"Not far from here, actually. New Haven."

"A little over an hour away," said Alex. "Not far, indeed. Fine. Now, Sebastian, what about this note you found?"

Sebastian explained about the three earlier notes that had been left for Michaele, and this last one.

"When Sebastian showed it to me," Michaele said, "I thought at first it meant that this secret admirer, whoever he is, was saying good-bye, but now I'm afraid . . . I'm afraid . . ."

"You're afraid this person has kidnapped your

son," said Alex Theopoulos. Michaele nodded.

"Do you think that's what's happened?" Katie asked Alex.

"Frankly," said Alex, "no."

Michaele looked up, relieved and disappointed at the same time. "But, then—"

"I think he's run away," Alex said. "That's what happens most often in cases like this. Did he have any reason to run away, Miss Caraway?"

Michaele moved slowly to the table and sat down. She asked for, and received, a cup of coffee. "He's been unhappy," she said at last. "I've been trying to wish it away, but I can't. I guess he misses his father terribly. Or perhaps he just isn't happy being with me."

"Or perhaps," said Jessica Hallem, "he just isn't happy."

Michaele looked up. "Perhaps," she said. "Whatever it is, I've begun to think seriously about asking his father to take him back."

Sebastian said softly, "Maybe he already has."

The room was suddenly still.

Michaele said. "You don't think Frank—"

"Sebastian has a point," said Alex. "Maybe your husband—"

"Ex-husband."

"Excuse me. Your ex-husband, perhaps he's come for the boy. Perhaps just for a visit. Or perhaps something more. Are you on good terms with Mr. —"

"Bishop. Frank Bishop. He manages rock groups. You may have heard of his hottest property. As they say. A group called Slam."

If Alex Theopoulos had knowledge of the latest rock sensation, he kept it to himself. "You haven't answered my question," he said.

"We're not on very good terms, no. But I don't think—"

"Why don't you call him? Where does he live?"

"He lives in New York City, but he's often out of town. He goes where his groups go."

"Why don't you try calling him now?" Alex suggested. Michaele looked at him. "At least we might clear up one loose end."

"All right." Michaele walked to the phone, picked up the receiver and dialed. After a moment, the tinny sound of a recorded message was heard. Michaele turned to the others. "There, you see?" she said. "It's his answering machine. The message says he's away for a few days. I'm sure he's on tour with Slam." She hung up abruptly.

"He's away," she said then. "Not home."

"He's away," said Alex Theopoulos.

Michaele shook her head. "I know what you're thinking, but it's impossible. He isn't here. He's on tour with Slam, that's all."

Alex let the matter go. Promising that he'd do

everything he could, unofficially, he bid everyone good night and went out to his car to begin searching the area. Josh and David Lepinsky left with him.

Sebastian had kept the information to himself, but he remembered reading that morning that Slam had just opened a one-week engagement at Madison Square Garden—in New York City.

26

"WE SHOULD be going too," Sally said several minutes later.

"Yes," said Dougie Scott, rising. "You're in the bosom of a loving family, Michaele. We shall not leave you unattended."

"Please don't go," Michaele said.

"We're serving no purpose here except to add unnecessarily to the somber mood. I'm sure Donovan will be home soon. It's getting dark now. He'll want to come back to his mother."

"Oh, Dougie, I hope you're right."

"Yes," he said, sucking in his breath, "so do I." Then, "Michaele, may I speak with you alone for a moment?"

"Of course."

The two left the room, the director reaching up slightly to place his arm around the actress's shoulders. Sally smiled at the others and said, "Well, I may as well have another cup of coffee. Make it an even dozen."

Sebastian excused himself. On his way up the stairs to his room, he overheard a bit of the conversation between Dougie and Michaele, who were in the living room. It was enough to make him stop and listen for more.

"It's not what either of us want," Dougie Scott was saying. "But perhaps it would be for the best."

"Drop out of the show? I can't do that. It wouldn't be fair to Cliff. Or to you. Or to anyone else, for that matter."

"You can't think about others now, Michaele. You must think of yourself. This trouble with Donovan, it clearly indicates some deeper trouble."

"*You* know Frank, Dougie. Do you think he'd steal Donovan away from me?"

"Frank's so unpredictable, I don't know what he'd do. I just know you're in trouble of some kind. All these mishaps aren't just coincidences, you know. I've really begun to think that the play *is* under an unlucky star."

There was a moment of silence. Then Dougie said, "If you won't quit the show, will you at least reconsider an understudy?"

"But why—"

"Please think about it. That's all I ask. With all that's happening, who knows what tomorrow holds in store?"

There was a longer silence. Then, Michaele said in a hoarse voice, worn with worry, "Do what you think is best."

Just then, Sebastian heard someone coming from the kitchen. He moved quickly up the stairs and into his room. Moments later, he looked out his window and saw the director and costume mistress walking down the sidewalk and toward their car. They turned and waved at someone inside. That someone was probably Michaele.

It was getting dark. Donovan was out there somewhere, Sebastian thought. Out there in the night.

27

AT NINE O'CLOCK, Donovan returned.

Sebastian heard Michaele's cry from his bedroom. He ran down the stairs, two at a time, to find Michaele on her knees in the front hall, her arms wrapped tightly around her son. Her crutches had fallen to either side. She was laughing or crying, Sebastian wasn't sure which.

Donovan's face was placid, so flat and unfathomable that it almost looked like its own reflection in a pool of murky water. He didn't have any cuts or scratches; he wasn't dirty; his clothes were barely mussed. It didn't appear that any harm had come to him. But where he had been remained a mystery.

When questioned, he simply shrugged and said that he had run away. When asked why, he simply shrugged.

"It doesn't matter," Michaele said, fighting back her tears and her anger. "The important thing is that you're home. And you're safe. Oh, Donovan, everyone was so worried about you."

"You?" Donovan said.

"Me? Of course I was worried about you. What do you think?"

"I don't know," said Donovan.

"Donovan," said Will Barth, "did someone take you from the theater?" The boy shook his head. "You left on your own?" He nodded. "Your father didn't come for you?"

Donovan's eyes flashed angrily at his mother. "No. I ran away."

"I'm sure Donovan and his mother have a lot to talk about," Katie said. "But first, how about something to eat, Donovan? You must be starved. We have lots of cold cuts. Shall I fix you a sandwich?"

While Katie prepared Donovan's meal, Will called Josh and Alex to tell them the good news. Michaele waited until she'd put her son to bed before calling Sally and Dougie.

She was exhausted as she spoke, but exuberant at the same time. "That's right," she told Dougie, "I'm doing the show. Of course. And *without* an understudy, love. No, Frank didn't have a thing to do with it. I think it's been hard for Donovan being in a strange, new place with a mom who's almost a stranger herself. I'm going to make it up to him, Dougie, I swear.

"But first we have a show to do. And now it's more important to me than ever. If we can make a go of it, love, we can move the play to New York.

[99]

And then I'll have loads of time to spend with Donovan. And he'll be living where he's comfortable and happy. My bad luck is behind me, love. I can feel it. Tomorrow is a new day."

28 WHEN MICHAELE arrived for rehearsal the next morning, she stopped by her dressing room before going onstage. The yellow roses had died. On the counter, she found a note, which read:

Something wicked this way comes.

29

" 'THAT GUY UPSTAIRS is a real jerk,' " Sebastian said.

" 'I wish you wouldn't talk about him that way,' " said Michaele.

" 'But, Mommy,' " Rachel said, " 'you just called him a nerd.' "

" 'A nerd is not the same as a jerk.' "

" 'What's the difference?' " said Sebastian.

"Sebastian, love," Dougie called out, "don't step on Michaele's line. You want to leave time for the audience to laugh."

"Isn't he an optimist?" Doris Carpenter said to Rob McGrath, loud enough for everyone to hear.

"All right, Michaele," said Dougie. "Take it from your line, 'A nerd is not the same . . .' "

Michaele wasn't listening. "I thought that was the end of him," she said aloud.

"Sorry, love, what was that?" said the director.

Michaele shook her head. "I'm sorry, Dougie. I'm having a hard time concentrating this morning. May we take a short break? I could use a few minutes."

"Of course."

During the break, Sebastian watched Mark come over to Michaele and put his arm about her shoulder. "What is it?" he said. "Tell Markie about it."

"I thought I'd heard the last of this admirer of mine," she replied. "Now, this." She pulled the latest note from her pocket and showed it to Mark.

Doris and Rob joined them. "What's the matter, Michaele?" Rob said. "Oh, another fan letter."

"Hardly," said Michaele. "This one sounds threatening."

"What's it say?" asked Liz Burke over Doris's shoulder.

Michaele started to read, " 'Something wicked—' "

"Don't," said Mark.

Michaele looked up, surprised. "It's a quote from the Scottish play," Mark explained. "Bad luck."

Michaele frowned. "Bad luck. When will it be behind me?"

"May I see it?" Sarah asked. Michaele handed her the note. "Oh, what pretty writing. I wish I could write like this. It's so . . . so creative."

"Me, too," said Liz.

"Creative," someone else said. "Huh! That isn't writing, it's *penmanship*." The others turned to see that Cliff Davies had joined them.

"Whatever it is," Michaele said, "it's frightening. I tell myself I'm surrounded by friends, yet—"

"You *are*," said Doris. "Everyone adores you, Michaele. I can't imagine who would do this to you."

"Someone with a sick sense of humor," Rob said.

"I don't think it's someone who's kidding around," said Cliff. "I think whoever it is means business."

"What do you mean?" Michaele asked. "Now you're really scaring me."

"Sorry, Michaele," said Cliff. "But face it. You inspire some pretty deep feelings in people. You can't help it, it's just who you are. Perhaps you've driven someone over the edge."

"That isn't funny," Mark Lawson said.

"I didn't intend it to be," said Cliff.

For a moment, it looked as if Mark and Cliff would lock horns once again. But in that moment, Dougie stepped into the circle and said, "Are you feeling better, Michaele? If so, I think we should get started."

"Yes, love," said Michaele, "I'd like that." She looked at the note in her hand, then lifted her eyes to see Sebastian watching her. She extended the note to him. "Evidence," she whispered.

Turning back, she looked out into the auditorium for Mintsy to tell her where they were to take it from. But the stage manager was not at her post. Instead, she stood at the door talking to Richard. Suddenly, the two looked up at Michaele. They looked worried.

"What is it?" Michaele asked. "What's wrong?"

Richard said something, but Michaele could not hear. "What?" she called. "What are you saying?"

"I'm sorry, Michaele," Mintsy said. "But it seems that Donovan has disappeared again."

30 THIS TIME, he hadn't gotten far. Sebastian spotted the boy sitting cross-legged on the ground near the main entrance to Siddons College.

"There he is," he called to the others.

Michaele, Dougie and Mintsy were within hearing distance. They came running.

When Donovan saw them rushing toward him, he scrambled to his feet but once up didn't move.

Michaele grabbed him by the shoulders and shook him. "Why are you doing this to me?" she cried.

Donovan's eyes welled up with tears. His face seemed to grow fat.

"Answer me," Michaele said sternly. "Why are you running away?"

"I'm n-not," he blubbered. He glanced behind him nervously.

"You're not?" Dougie said. "But you told your mother—"

"I'm not supposed to t-tell. I . . . I . . ."

Michaele loosened the grip she had on her son.

"What aren't you supposed to tell?" she said. "Were you to meet someone here?"

Donovan began to speak, then looked again over his shoulder and tightened his lips resolutely.

"Who asked you to meet him here?" Michaele said. "Was it a man? Was it someone you know?"

When Donovan remained silent, Michaele tightened her grip. "You listen to me, young man," she said. "This is serious. I want to know right now who you were meeting here."

Dougie said, "The boy is frightened, Michaele. Perhaps—"

Though Donovan's answer was barely more than a whisper, it stopped Dougie from saying another word. "Daddy," he said.

Mintsy and Dougie exchanged a glance.

"Daddy wanted you to meet him here? I don't understand. How did you . . . how did he—"

"He called me on the telephone in the theater office," Donovan said, his voice shaking. "He said if I met him here he'd spend the day with me."

"So you came," said Michaele. "But what about yesterday? Were you to meet Daddy then, too?"

Donovan's tears erupted like a long awaited rain. Michaele took him in her arms. "It's all right," she said soothingly. "It's all right."

When at last he could speak, Donovan told his mother, "He said he'd come yesterday. But he never did. I waited and waited, but he never came. So I ran away."

"Why, Donovan?"

"Nobody loves me," the boy said simply.

Michaele said, "Is that what you think?"

"Nobody loves me," said Donovan. "Nobody wants me."

31

WHEN THE CAST broke for lunch, Michaele called her ex-husband's number in New York. To her surprise, he answered the phone.

"You haven't been anywhere near Pembroke in the last few days?" Sebastian heard her say. "You swear you haven't? You haven't called Donovan? No, Frank, I'm not accusing you of anything. Something's going on here, that's all. And I'm worried."

"Did he explain why the message on his answering machine said he was out of town?" Sebastian asked Michaele when she'd gotten off the phone.

Michaele nodded. "Things were so crazy with the Slam concert opening, he didn't want to have to worry about returning calls. That sounds like something Frank would do. So. Where does that leave us? Donovan is lying, I guess. Or Frank." Michaele shook her head. "I don't know what to think anymore."

"Maybe neither of them is lying," Sebastian said.

"What do you mean?"

"What if somebody is pretending to be Donovan's dad?"

"But why would someone do that?" said Michaele. "Do you think someone really wants to kidnap him?" There was something in her eyes that made her look like a little girl in a fairy tale, lost in a dark forest and afraid to let herself sleep. "If someone wanted to scare me," she said, "they've succeeded. But they'll have a fight on their hands, love. I'll die before I let anything happen to Donovan."

32

AFTER MICHAELE left to have lunch with her son, Sebastian went to his dressing room. For the first time that day, he was alone.

Digging into his paper-bag lunch, he began to think about the events of the past few days. First, there were the notes. He pulled the one Michaele had given him from his pocket and looked at it.

If music be the food of love, play on.

He then studied the one she'd received that day.

Something wicked this way comes.

What did the change mean? he wondered. Why would someone in love with Michaele suddenly turn threatening? If everyone loved her, and it seemed that everyone did, then who would want to hurt her? And what would be accomplished if they succeeded? What was the relationship between the "accidents" that had befallen Michaele and the attempted kidnapping, if that's what it was, of her son? There were many unanswered questions.

He looked into the mirror as if it might hold an answer. But it merely reflected his own puzzled expression. He took a bite of his sandwich and thought about the few clues he had. They were so meager, and the conclusions he had drawn so few.

A tall, red-haired boy of sixteen or seventeen had bought a dozen yellow roses for Michaele. There were no red-haired boys among the apprentices. Perhaps one of the summer students at the college was the secret admirer, Sebastian thought. But would a stranger have been able to come and go so easily without having been noticed? No, it seemed more likely that the redhead, whoever he was, had been a messenger for someone else.

The sound of the shoes he'd heard in the hall, he'd realized, was made by metal taps. He'd listened for the same sound since and hadn't heard it at all. He'd even brought tap dancing into the conversation during a break recently, but that had proved inconclusive. Mark had said he'd taken lessons when he was a child, but hadn't put on a pair of tap shoes in years. Rob and Doris, Liz and Sarah, even Dougie had acknowledged some experience with tap dancing at one time or another in their lives. But none were doing it now.

What if it was the tall, redheaded kid who had taps on his shoes?

Whoever it was clearly knew some facts about Michaele Caraway. He knew that she was superstitious, but that fact had quickly become common knowledge. He knew one of her favorite foods, her favorite flower, her favorite piece of music. He knew what would please her . . . and what would frighten her.

He knew Shakespeare well enough to quote from his plays. He knew how to write using calligraphy. He knew how to remove a bolt from a chair.

And, of course, *he* could be a *she*.

Sebastian reached for a piece of paper to write down what he knew and what he needed to know. As he did, he again caught sight of his reflection in the mirror. Did he have the makings of a real actor? he wondered. Michaele had said he did. She had started to say something else. That there was a way he—something. She'd been interrupted. Perhaps he'd never know. Unless he asked her. Yes, he'd ask her what she saw in him that showed he had the makings of a real actor. But first he'd save her. Like Harrison Ford in *The Seventh Skull*, he'd rescue her from perils dark and dangerous. Even if he had to do it single-handedly. Even if, like Harrison Ford, he ran the risk of falling in love along the way.

Sebastian smiled at himself in the mirror. The smile was tough, but tender.

"I don't believe it," he heard someone say. He jerked his head around to see Corrie and David standing in the doorway. "We've been looking all over for you" David went on, "and where do we find you? In your dressing room making faces at yourself in the mirror! You're getting worse than Rachel, Sebastian."

"We were putting some of the flats up on the stage," Corrie said. "We thought maybe you'd help."

Sebastian looked away. "I wanted to be alone. I needed to think about . . . things."

"Were you working on the case?" David said.

"In a way."

David came over and straddled a chair next to Sebastian's. Corrie leaned against the door. "So," David said, "what have you figured out?"

"Not much. It's baffling."

"Baffling?" said David. "Where'd you come up with a word like baffling?"

Sebastian said nothing. "Can you tell us what you *have* figured out?" Corrie asked.

"Well, I . . . I, uh . . ." Sebastian wasn't sure why, but he didn't feel like sharing his thoughts with his friends just then. He was wishing for an excuse to get away when one came his way.

"Sebastian," said Michaele, passing the open door. Donovan was at her side. "I've just asked Rachel to come to my dressing room to run lines with me. Will you join us? We can do our family scenes."

"Sure," Sebastian said, crumpling up the remains of his lunch and tossing them in a wastebasket.

[114]

"See you guys later," he said to Corrie and David. And he was out the door.

"Gee," Corrie said, "that was weird. Almost like he didn't want to talk with us."

"Yeah," said David a little sadly. "Almost like he doesn't need us anymore."

33

A NEW NOTE awaited Michaele in her dressing room. "Two in one day," she said drily, spotting it on the counter. "Aren't I lucky?" She opened it and read,

> *"One woe doth tread upon another's heel*
> *so fast they follow.*

"I'd laugh if I weren't so terrified," Michaele said. She looked at her son and said, more to herself than anyone else, "What does he want from me? What does he want?" Donovan returned his mother's worried look with a blank stare.

Suddenly, Rachel bounded into the room. "Michaele," she said, "will you help me with something?"

"Sure, angel, if I can."

"I'm trying to decide on a stage name. Which do you like better—*Danielle* or *Cyndi* Somerset?"

"PLACES FOR ACT ONE, please," Mintsy Jones called out at the top of the afternoon rehearsal.

Backstage, Michaele stood alone for a moment, apart from her stage son and daughter. She was lost in her own thoughts, Sebastian knew, preparing herself mentally to become the character she was to portray. It was an actor's technique, she had explained, and he had learned not to interrupt her.

He saw her take something out of her pocket. By now, he knew what it was. It was the bent nail he'd seen her rubbing at the first rehearsal and at the beginning of each rehearsal since. Her good luck nail, she called it. It was the first nail she'd hammered as an apprentice when she was a teenager. She'd joked that her carpentry skills had forced her into acting. She closed her eyes and stood stock-still, leaning on her crutches. When Mintsy called, "Lights up," she opened her eyes, winked at Sebastian and Rachel, and said "Let's go, kids."

She was Heather Dexter now. And she was Heather Dexter when she went to straighten a picture frame on the back wall of the set moments later. Then she heard Mintsy scream, "Watch out!"

Sebastian pulled her away, crutches and all, just as the wall crashed to the ground. It was not Heather Dexter who stared at the fallen piece of scenery in shocked disbelief. It was Michaele Caraway. It was the little girl in the fairy tale, lost and tired but afraid to fall asleep.

34

SEBASTIAN AND THE REST of the cast weren't called until two o'clock the next day. The morning call was for the apprentices only, a technical rehearsal to practice the lighting and sound cues, the changing of properties and scenery. Sebastian came to watch.

"Look who's here," David said to Corrie, as Sebastian took a seat next to his two friends in the auditorium. "The actor."

"How's the investigation going?" Corrie asked, without looking up.

"Not so great," Sebastian said. "I was hoping maybe I'd find something out by coming here today."

"You'll find out how hard us techies work," David said.

Sebastian glanced at David and Corrie, scrunched up in their seats, their knees resting against the seat backs in front of them. "Yeah, I see," he said.

Corrie grunted. "Not now, Sebastian. They're doing light cues. They don't need us yet. But you should see how hard we work when the props get changed. That's our job."

"Listen," Sebastian said, "did Richard figure out

what happened with that wall yesterday?"

"It's like the chair," David said, turning to face Sebastian. "And the stairs. Somebody messed with the pin hinges that hold the flats together. As soon as Michaele touched that picture frame, the thing started to fall. There was nothing holding it up, see."

Sebastian watched areas of light well up and fade away as Mintsy Jones called out the cues for the light changes. The effect was eerie. It was as if he were seeing the stage set come slowly and uncertainly to life. A lamp came on suddenly in the downstairs living room. "Not cue forty-two," Mintsy shouted. "Forty-one!"

"Sebastian," David whispered. "I found something interesting. Come on."

Sebastian followed David and Corrie to the scenery shop. No one was there. David went immediately to a row of lockers, knelt down, reached under one and pulled out a magazine. He handed it to Sebastian.

"Look at page one-seventeen," he said.

" 'I Love Life,' Says Actress Michaele Caraway," the article was headed. Sebastian flipped to the front cover. It was a dogeared copy of *McCall's*. "This magazine is five years old," he said. "Where'd it come from?"

"I just found it here," said David. "The thing that's interesting is this." He took the magazine away from Sebastian and leafed through it until he found what he was looking for. "Read this," he said, handing it back.

Sebastian read aloud. " 'I have so many favorite things: jogging at dawn, listening to Bach, taking long, lazy baths. I adore macadamia nuts and yellow roses; sweet, sentimental songs like "Greensleeves"; long-haired, sad-eyed dogs; pizza with all the extras.' Whose magazine is this?"

"We don't know," said Corrie. "It wasn't in one of the lockers. It was on the floor there, hidden almost. We thought maybe—"

"Sshh," Sebastian said. He turned toward the door. Someone was coming.

To his amazement, a tall red-haired boy entered the scenery shop. "Who's that?" Sebastian said in a hushed voice.

"Beats me," said David. "I never saw him before."

"He's the one."

"What do you mean? Oh, yeah! The kid who bought the flowers."

"Are you looking for somebody?" Sebastian asked.

"Yeah," said the stranger. "I'm looking for the technical director. Isn't he supposed to be here?"

"Richard? He's in the theater right now," David said. "How come you're looking for him?"

It was then Sebastian noticed that the teenager was carrying a pair of shoes in his hands. Holding them up, the boy said, "I have his shoes. He's staying with us, see, and he left his good shoes at the house this morning. He asked me to drop them off. You said he's in the theater?"

"Yeah," said Sebastian, walking toward the boy. "But he's really busy right now. We're going over there. We can take them for you."

"Thanks a lot," said the boy. "I need to get going anyway."

"Sure," Sebastian said, taking the shoes from him. "No problem."

As soon as the boy had gone, Sebastian turned the shoes over in his hands. He was not surprised to see that there were taps on the heels and tips. "His good shoes," he said. "The good shoes he wore to bring a music box to Michaele Caraway." Looking at the magazine in David's hand, he said, "I guess we've found out who that belongs to."

"Yeah," Corrie said, "*and* who Michaele's secret admirer is."

Sebastian nodded.

"And who's been playing all those dirty tricks on her," said David, shaking his head. "I can't believe it's Richard. He's such a nice guy."

"I'm not sure yet that it is," said Sebastian.

"Huh?" David said. "I don't get it."

"While you guys are busy changing props, I'm going to keep tabs on Richard. There's more to this than meets the eye."

35

SEBASTIAN WATCHED RICH-
ARD carefully all the rest of the
morning. But as two o'clock ap-
proached and with it the arrival of the actors for the
afternoon rehearsal, the technical director had done
nothing more suspicious than leave the auditorium
several times. Each time Sebastian had followed him.
Right into the men's room.

"I've had too much coffee," Richard said to Sebastian the third time he found himself at an adjoin-
ing urinal. "What's your problem?"

"Nerves," Sebastian replied. He smiled weakly.

"Not having much luck, are you?" Corrie asked
at lunch.

Sebastian shook his head. He was watching
Richard share his lunch with Sally under a nearby
elm. "That doesn't mean anything, though," he said.
"All it takes—wait a minute."

Richard stood, brushed off his pants and turned
toward the theater.

"He's going back to work," David said.

"Or to the men's room," said Sebastian. "That

guy has the weakest bladder around. I'm going to follow him."

"Can I go with you?" Corrie asked.

Sebastian wavered a moment, then smiled. "Only as far as the men's room door," he said.

But Richard was not headed for the men's room this time. He was walking slowly down the hall along the dressing rooms. When he was only a few feet from Michaele Caraway's door, he turned and looked anxiously behind him. Sebastian, David and Corrie ducked into an open doorway.

A moment later, they were outside the star's dressing room. Sebastian peeked in and saw Richard seated at the makeup counter. He held an envelope in his hand.

"What are you doing?" Sebastian asked.

Richard dropped the envelope to the floor and looked up. "Nothing," he said, surprised. "I just . . . nothing."

"You're the one," said Sebastian.

" 'The one'? What are you talking about? Never mind that. Why are you following me, lad? What's going on?"

"You know," Sebastian said. "You're the one who's been leaving those messages for Michaele and sending her roses and macadamia nuts. And scaring her."

"I didn't mean to scare her," Richard said. "I swear."

"So you admit it."

Flustered, Richard looked away. "No, I . . . I . . . Oh, what's the use? It's all up now, anyway." He stared at the card on the floor.

"If you didn't mean to hurt Michaele, then why have you been doing these things to her?" Sebastian asked.

"I would never harm Miss Caraway," Richard said slowly. His words seemed to be addressed more to himself—or to some unseen presence in the room—than to Sebastian and his friends. "I . . . admire her, you might say. Though 'worship' might be the better word. Do you know I've seen every film she's ever made? And when she acted on the stage, I saw her plays time and time again. I would have given anything to work with her, would have done anything to be near her. As it turned out, I didn't have to do much."

"What do you mean?" Sebastian asked.

"I was offered a job in New Haven, one that ordinarily I would have accepted in a flash. Instead, I called Brian Butterworth—he was the technical director here—and told him about it. I said I could help him get it, and I did. Then, knowing there would be a vacancy here, I called my old friend Sally. We go back a long way, Sally and I. I called her just to say hello. At least, that's what I told her. When she offered me the job here, I pretended to be surprised. But I wasn't, of course. Because I'd masterminded the whole thing, you see. And here I am."

"And you started sending Michaele some of her favorite things," said Sebastian. "Things you'd read about in a magazine you'd carried around for five years."

"I know it was immature, obsessive even," Richard said. "But I was in love. What can I tell you?"

"Then why did you threaten her?" David asked.

Richard looked up. There was a look of anguish on his face. That look turned suddenly to one of surprise, then to deeper anguish. Michaele Caraway was standing in the doorway.

"I'd like an answer to that question, too," she said. "I've heard everything, Richard. Everything but when your love turned to hate. And why you're trying to hurt me."

"But I'm not," Richard said. He thrust out his open hands as if offering up his innocence. "When I wrote you that note, the one that said 'Parting is such sweet sorrow,' I meant just that. I was saying goodbye. I realized just how foolish I'd been. But I've never hated you. These latest messages, these threats, they're not mine. I didn't write them."

"Then why are you in my dressing room?"

Richard picked up the fallen note. "I came to take this away. I knew someone else was leaving you these notes. I knew how they were upsetting you. I wanted to put a stop to it."

"May I see it?" Michaele asked. Richard handed

her the note, and Michaele read, " 'I must be cruel only to be kind.' " With a sigh, she said, "What a perverse mind. I believe you, Richard. I believe you're not the one. But I'm still curious. What became of my secret admirer?"

"I still admire you," Richard said softly. "But I was obsessed with a love that couldn't be. And then I discovered one that could."

Michaele looked puzzled. "Meaning?" she said.

"Meaning me," said another accented voice. Everyone turned to see Sally standing behind Michaele, a dress draped over her arm. She touched Michaele's shoulder and said, "Richard found that there was more love to be had in an old friendship than in a secret passion. He told me everything, Michaele. He wanted to confess it all to you, but I advised him to keep quiet. I didn't want you to think he meant you any harm. It's better, though. Better to have it out in the open."

"Forgive me," Richard said to Michaele. "I was a fool in love with a dream."

Michaele smiled wearily. "You're not a fool," she said. "And I'm not a dream. I do forgive you. Only—"

"Only there's still someone," Sebastian said.

"Yes," said Michaele. "Someone who wants to hurt me. Who? Who is it?"

Gently, Sebastian lifted the card from Michaele's hand. He studied it for a moment.

[126]

I must be cruel only to be kind.

All at once he was sure he knew. He wondered why it hadn't been clear a long time ago. The only question left was what cruelty lay ahead. And how he could prevent it from happening.

36

IT WAS THREE O'CLOCK. Dress rehearsal was about to begin.

"I've lost it," Michaele muttered. "I can't find it anywhere."

"What?" Doris asked.

"My nail."

The cast was sitting in the green room, that backstage lounge where actors gather while waiting to go on. Everyone was listening.

"Your nail?" said Rob.

"My good luck nail," Michaele said. "I keep it in my makeup case. Now it's gone. I'm no good without it."

"Would someone have taken it?" Doris said.

"I don't know. But I don't know a lot of things these days."

Just then, the director entered the room.

"Now, children," said Dougie, "despite the theatrical tradition that the worse the dress rehearsal the better the opening night, I want you to go out there and give it your all. Michaele, love, where are your crutches?"

"The doctor told me I could use a cane," Michaele said. "It's not my crutches I miss right now. It's my nail."

Dougie cocked his head and started to speak when Mintsy opened the door behind him.

"Two minutes, everyone," she said. "Did you tell them, Dougie?"

"Tell them?"

"About Frank Rich."

The actors buzzed excitedly at the mention of the well-known theater critic.

"Is he coming to the opening?" asked Mark.

"I didn't want to say anything," Dougie said.

Mintsy clapped a hand over her mouth. "Sorry," she said. "I thought you were going to tell them."

"We're going to be in *The New York Times*," said Liz. "I'm going to be famous."

"Oh my god," Michaele said. "I'm not ready for critics. Dougie, isn't there any way to stop it? Later in the run, perhaps, but not so soon."

Dougie knelt by the actress's side. "You'll be fine," he said reassuringly. "By opening night, you'll have nothing to worry about."

"If only I hadn't lost that nail."

"You don't need a good luck piece. You have everything you need inside you."

"I don't know," Michaele said. "With all that's happened—"

"Places for Act One," Mintsy called out. "Good luck, everyone."

Michaele no longer remembered what it was she was going to say.

37 OPENING NIGHT CAME at last and with it all the anxieties Sebastian had anticipated but not yet felt. Would he forget his lines? Would he be able to keep his mind on the play and not be distracted by his family sitting in the third row?

Would Michaele be all right?

Staring into his dressing room mirror, he tried to shut out the sounds around him—Rob McGrath singing a country-and-western song; Buster Wingate chattering on to no one about a whale named Roscoe; other actors in other rooms laughing and singing and wishing each other luck—in order to concentrate on the task of applying his makeup.

But then there came a sound he could not shut out.

It was the sound of panic, the sound of fear. And it came from Michaele's dressing room. He heard her pounding on her door. He heard her cry, "I'm locked in! Please! Somebody, open the door!" It's happened, he thought. The final cruelty.

Sebastian and Rob bolted from the room.

Gathered outside Michaele's dressing room were

Doris, Liz and Sarah, Mark, Cliff, and Dougie. Dougie shook the doorknob fiercely, but to no avail. "It won't budge," he said to the others. "Try to relax!" he called out to Michaele. "We'll get help."

"I won't be able to stand it in here much longer, Dougie," Michaele said, her voice starting to tremble. "I'm . . . I feel closed in. Please hurry. I can't . . . can't breathe."

"We'll hurry, love," Dougie said. "We'll get Richard here right away."

Others had joined the group now. Rachel was there, Buster, Sally, David and Corrie, some of the other apprentices. And someone Sebastian had never seen before. She was tall and blonde and very, very pretty. She was about Michaele's age, he guessed. In fact, she looked something like Michaele. The last piece suddenly fell into place. It was clear now that he was right. He knew who had been terrifying Michaele. He didn't completely understand why, and he wasn't sure he'd be able to prove it. But he knew who it was.

"Can one of you get Richard?" Dougie asked the apprentices. "Or, better still, does anyone know how to open this door?"

"A key would help," Doris said. Several people laughed, more out of nervousness than amusement.

"I'll find Richard," said Corrie.

"Of course a key would help," Dougie said. "But there doesn't seem to be one."

From behind Michaele's door came the sound of crying.

"Let me talk to her," said Cliff, shoving Dougie aside. "Michaele? Michaele?"

"What?" she asked sharply.

"Are you all right?"

"My god, Cliff, what a stupid question. Isn't it obvious I'm not all right? I'm terrified. I can't stand being closed in. You know that. Please, Cliff, just get someone to open the door."

"We're getting Richard," said Cliff. "Michaele, tell me what happened."

Michaele sounded as if she were trying to control her tears. "I don't know," she said. "I left my door open, as I always do. Then all of a sudden it slammed shut. When I tried to open it, I couldn't. It was stuck or locked or something."

Cliff looked at the door. "It doesn't seem like the kind that would lock by itself," he said. "Did you *hear* it lock, Michaele? Did you hear the key turn?"

"I don't . . . I don't know, Cliff. I've got to lie down. I'm getting dizzy. I'm not going to be able to do the show tonight. I can't after this. It's useless."

Richard appeared suddenly. "Corrie told me everything," he said, moving quickly to the door. He looked it over quickly. "Damn. The hinges are on the inside. There must be a key. Where would there be keys to these doors?"

No one said anything. Sebastian listened to the

sound of Michaele's ragged breathing. It was time for action. He would have to take a chance now, a big one, but he wasn't sure there was any other way. He opened his mouth and said, "Dougie has the key."

The director's jaw dropped. "What . . . what are you talking about?" he sputtered.

"Don't you remember that time in Michaele's dressing room?" Sebastian said. "You were there, remember? With David and Michaele and me? She said she was afraid of being shut inside such a small room. And you told her not to worry, that you'd always keep the key in case anything happened." He looked into Dougie's eyes to see if the director believed his story, which was, of course, a lie built on some truth. Dougie hadn't been there, but Sebastian was sure he'd overheard everything from outside the room.

"Is that true?" Richard asked. "Do you have it?"

"Well, I . . . I . . . no, of course not. I never said that."

"Sure you did," said Sebastian, gathering courage as he spoke. "You said you'd never let anything bad happen to Michaele. You'd protect her, you said."

There was silence as Dougie stared at Sebastian in confusion. "Well, I do want to protect her," he said. "That's what I'm doing. Isn't it? I . . . I . . ."

"So give Richard the key," Sebastian said. "You probably forgot you had it. It's in your pocket."

The silence was longer this time. Everyone looked to Dougie to see what he would do.

He watched the faces watching him. "I . . . yes, yes, I have it here," he said at last, digging into his jacket pocket. His hands were shaking noticably. "I'm getting the key, Michaele," he called out. "Are you all right, love?"

There was no answer.

As Dougie pulled the key from his pocket, something came with it and fell to the ground. Sebastian saw what it was. So did the others. Michaele's good-luck nail lay at Dougie's feet.

Richard turned the key in the lock and pushed open the door. Michaele was sitting on the edge of the bed, her face white and drawn. Richard knelt by her side. "It's all right now," he told her.

She turned from him and stared at Dougie. "It isn't," she said. "It isn't all right. All this time, I thought you were on my side, Dougie. You helped me believe in myself. You told me you were my friend. But it was all a lie, wasn't it?" She looked down and saw her bent nail lying on the floor. Her eyes welled up with tears. "It came to me," she said. "The sound of the key turning in the lock came to me, Dougie. You locked me in here, knowing what it would do to me. You're the one who's been trying to hurt me all along. Well, you've succeeded. You've hurt me. Perhaps not in the way you intended, but you've hurt me deeply."

[135]

Dougie started to speak, but Michaele wouldn't let him.

"I don't want to hear anything you have to say," she said, rising from the daybed. Color had returned to her face. "I don't want to hear you or see you. I have a performance to give tonight. I must get ready to become Heather Dexter. And Heather Dexter has never heard of Dougie Scott, love. For her, Dougie Scott does not exist." She gave Dougie a piercing look, sat down at her mirror, and picked up a makeup sponge.

The crowd dispersed in silence. The director stood alone, the bent nail at his feet. From a couple of yards away, the tall, blonde woman looked at him with a puzzled expression. When Sebastian turned to go back to his dressing room, he was left with Dougie's ashen face in his mind's eye. And he wondered if he had done the right thing.

38

" 'AND WE HAVE FIVE KIDS,' " Michaele said.

" 'Don't let a little thing like that worry you,' " said Mark. " 'You're forgetting—we also have five bathrooms!' "

The actors' embrace was followed by the sound of five toilets flushing, which in turn was followed by the sound of laughter and applause. The curtain fell, and the applause grew louder.

"We did it!" Mintsy Jones cried out. The actors hugged and kissed and ran to their places for the curtain call.

When it was Sebastian's turn to take a bow, he felt his legs begin to tremble. He stepped forward, listening to the applause as if he'd never heard the sound before. The *noise* it made. And it was all for him. In the split second before he bowed, he looked out at his family for the first time. When he saw their radiant smiles, he broke into one of his own.

He felt so alive he didn't know whether to laugh or to cry.

39

"POOR DOUGIE," Michaele said the next morning over breakfast.

"Poor you, you mean," said Jessica Hallem, passing a basket of muffins. "The man is not all there, if you ask me."

"To think of all he put you through," said Katie. "Frightening you, injuring you, making you think Donovan had been kidnapped. I still don't understand how he pulled that one off." Donovan, worn out from the party the night before, was still upstairs in bed.

"He called Donovan, pretending to be his father," Michaele said. "He wanted him to disappear for a few hours, just to worry me."

"Well, he succeeded," Will said.

Michaele nodded. "He hadn't counted on Donovan running away for as long as he did, though. That frightened him."

"But how did he fool Donovan in the first place?"

It was Sebastian who spoke up now. "He's good at voices. Remember how he imitated those actors on my show?"

"He called Frank's phone number in New York

and listened to his voice on the answering machine," said Michaele.

Jessica shook her head in amazement. "And do you mean to tell me," she said, "that he's the one who fixed it so that the chair would fall apart and that you'd slip on the stairs?"

"Yes. And so the flat would fall on me, too."

"He fixed those things when everyone else was on a break and out of the theater," said Sebastian. "Then, when we came back, he made sure Michaele was the first one to use whatever he'd fixed. When I'd figured out that it wasn't Richard who was after Michaele, I began to think about who had that kind of control. And the answer, of course, was Dougie."

"But why?" said Katie. "He said he was only concerned with your welfare, Michaele. Why would he undermine it?"

Michaele looked away, then turned back to the family. "We talked about it for hours last night," she said. "He told me everything, and whether you can understand this or not, I've forgiven him. He feels terrible about the anguish he's caused me."

"As well he should," Jessica said.

"Dougie really loves me," Michaele said. "What he did, he did out of love."

"You're going to have to explain that one," said Will.

"I'll try. Dougie had doubts about the play from the beginning. The only reason he agreed to direct it was because I was going to be in it. He needed to make a comeback of his own, you see. And with my name attached, he thought the play might be a hit. But after the first run-through, he was sure it would bomb. He didn't have enough confidence in himself or in Cliff to save the play, and he was convinced that I'd be devastated by its failure. So, even if everyone else was brought down, he decided to save me from ruin.

"For some reason I'll probably never understand, he thought the best course was to get me to drop out. When he overheard my reaction to David's whistling in the dressing room, he remembered how superstitious I am. The next day, he set up that little mishap with the chair. He hoped I'd connect it with the whistling, which, of course, I did.

"The following day, he purposely brought up the Scottish play. Mark's quoting one of its lines was a bit of serendipity. It just paved the way for his mentioning the title *and*, quite by chance, put a little suspicion on Mark, for anyone who might have been paying attention. He then put the grease on the steps."

"Didn't he know you'd be hurt?" said Katie.

"I don't think he really thought out the consequences," Michaele said. "He felt terrible each time I was injured. But that didn't stop him from striking again. After all, his aim was to get me to leave the play. And he wasn't going to stop until he'd succeeded. If that meant a fake kidnapping and bodily harm, then that's what it meant. When Richard stopped leaving me his little love notes, Dougie took it up, hoping he'd frighten me into believing there was a maniac on the loose. When I wasn't frightened, he *became* the maniac of his own imagination. He was desperate. Desperate and in love."

"He was so sure he'd get Michaele to drop out," Sebastian said, "that he went ahead and hired an understudy without letting anybody know. She was all set to take Michaele's place." He was referring to the tall, blonde woman who had appeared mysteriously at the theater the night before.

"His desperate last effort almost succeeded where the others had failed. He counted on my claustrophobia last night. But he hadn't counted on Sebastian."

Jessica looked proudly at her grandson. "What made you so sure that he was the culprit?" she asked.

"I wasn't really *sure*," said Sebastian. "But I had a pretty strong hunch. I knew that the person who had sent Michaele those first four notes wasn't the same one who sent the last three. For one thing, the notes became threatening. For another, there was a change in the handwriting. The first person knew how to write calligraphy; the other was copying. That made me start to think that it could have been two different people all along—one who loved Michaele, the other who wanted to hurt her. The problem was that *everybody* seemed to love Michaele. Nobody had the motive. But when I saw that last card, the one that said, 'I must be cruel only to be kind,' I began to wonder: who would hurt Michaele out of kindness?

"I thought it might be Dougie then and, putting it together with a few other things I knew, he was the obvious answer."

"What other things?" said Will.

"Well, the fact that when he was interviewed on my show, he avoided talking about the play. He really didn't want the play to get much attention, see. And the fact that he was the one to suggest to Michaele that she have an understudy . . . and that she consider dropping out of the play. Also, Dougie mentioned Michaele's being upset about David's whistling in the dressing room. He hadn't been in the room when that had happened, but I had a feeling he'd been listening at the door. I thought it was strange that he brought it up. Even stranger that he mentioned the Scottish play, knowing what a bad omen it was."

"That's the wonderful thing about being a director," Michaele said. "You have such control. Even when you're out of control."

" 'Poor Dougie' is right," said Katie. "What he put you through just because he loved you."

Michaele sipped her coffee slowly. Putting down her cup, she said, "The theater is full of illusions.

[142]

Those of us who work in it sometimes believe our illusions to be real or, as I once told Sebastian, we want what we can't have because we believe we can have everything. Apparently, Dougie has always loved me in a way I couldn't love him back. He believed that by saving me, he could earn my love. Frightening me may seem an odd way to express one's love, but to Dougie it made perfect sense. And it was real. Cliff believed he loved me, too, but he really loves only himself and his image of himself as a suffering artist. Richard was in love with someone he knew only through movies and magazine articles. Fortunately, he found the real thing in Sally.

"I had an illusion I believed in too. It was about you, Sebastian."

Sebastian looked up, surprised. "About me?" he said.

"Yes. I saw in you the son I wished I'd had. But that wasn't fair to you or to me. And it certainly wasn't fair to Donovan. You may have wonderful qualities, love, but you've had many advantages—advantages Donovan never had, even with his rich and famous mom and dad. I'm going to work very hard to give him those advantages now. I just hope I'm not too late."

Katie reached across the table and touched Michaele's hand. "You're not," she said.

There was a knock on the front door, followed by calls of hello.

[143]

"We're in the kitchen," Will shouted.

Josh Lepinsky came in, followed by Rachel and David and Corrie Wingate. He was waving a newspaper in his hands.

"The first review is in!" he cried.

"Read it," Sebastian said. Then he looked uncertainly at Michaele.

"Yes," she said, "read it. I'm ready for anything at this point."

"It starts out, '*The House of Cards*—Condemned Property.' "

Everyone groaned. "I think we're in trouble," said Michaele.

"Not everyone," Josh said. "Not you." He read, " 'Michaele Caraway could not have chosen a shakier property than the cardboard thin *House of Cards* for her return to the stage. Despite the valiant efforts of top-notch director Douglas Scott, the play is silly, shallow and pointless. Still, there was reason to rejoice last night. Michaele Caraway is a major star, whose talent, like her beauty, shines glowingly, regardless of her surroundings. Clearly, she has not lost her gift for stage acting. Let us hope she will not be discouraged by this ill-fated venture and will come home soon to Broadway.' "

"That's wonderful," Katie said.

"Yes, but poor Cliff."

"Is there anything about me?" Sebastian said.

"I was hoping you'd ask," David said, grabbing

[144]

the newspaper out of his father's hands. " 'Miss Caraway's children are played by the adorable Bambi Somerset and the tall and angular Sebastian Barth.' "

"Tall and angular?" said Sebastian. "That's it?"

The phone rang. Josh picked it up and handed it to Michaele. "It's Cliff," he said. "He wants to talk with you."

"Oh, the poor angel. What can I say?" She took the phone.

"Read the whole review, Josh," Katie said. "We don't need to listen in on Michaele's conversation."

David passed the paper back to his father who began to read. Sebastian did not hear what Josh was saying, however. All he could think about were the words "tall and angular." They didn't seem much upon which to build a theatrical career.

"Read that part about me being adorable again," Rachel was saying.

"It doesn't say you're adorable," said Josh. "It says Bambi Somerset is adorable. Whoever she is."

"Oh, Dad."

Michaele hung up the phone and laughed.

"Isn't he upset?" Jessica asked.

"Not in the least. In fact, he doesn't even seem to care. His agent called him this morning to tell him he's been offered the chance to write a movie script. He's leaving for Hollywood tomorrow."

Rachel asked. "Is there a part for me?"

"If you like bugs," Michaele said.

"If I like bugs?" said Rachel. "What's the movie?"

"*Insectivore II.*"

Everyone joined Michaele's laughter. "I'm going upstairs to wake Donovan," she said. "It looks like it's going to be a beautiful day. I think I'll spend it with my son."

Sebastian watched Michaele walk out of the room. He felt a little sad to see her go, though he wasn't sure why. Corrie smiled at him as if she understood. After a moment, he smiled back.

"Gee, Sebastian," David said, "now that you're a famous actor, I hope you're not too tall and angular to spend some time with your friends."

"Of course not," said Sebastian, grabbing a Frisbee from the kitchen counter. "Come on, big guy. What'd you say we go outside and toss this thing around?"